THE COLDEST NIGHT

The Coldest Night

A NOVEL BY

ROBERT OLMSTEAD

ALGONQUIN BOOKS OF CHAPEL HILL   2012

Published by
Algonquin Books of Chapel Hill
Post Office Box 2225
Chapel Hill, North Carolina 27515-2225

a division of
Workman Publishing
225 Varick Street
New York, New York 10014

LIBRARY OF CONGRESS CATALOGING-IN-PUBLICATION DATA
Olmstead, Robert.
Cold dark night : a novel / by Robert Olmstead. — First edition.
pages cm
ISBN 978-1-61620-043-5
1. Teenage boys — Fiction.   2. Life change events — Fiction.
3. Soldiers — Fiction.   4. Americans — Korea — Fiction.
5. Korean War, 1950–1953 — Fiction.   I. Title.
PS3565.L67C65 2012
813'.54 — dc23   2011045515

10 9 8 7 6 5 4 3 2 1
First Edition

THE COLDEST NIGHT

Part I

From whose womb comes the ice?
And the frost of heaven, who gives it birth?

The waters harden like stone,
And the surface of the deep is frozen.

JOB 38:29–30

Chapter 1

B Y 1941 THERE WAS little left to cut along the Elk and by then much of the land was sold to the government for National Forest. That February was a twenty-seven-inch snowfall on the mountain. The snow lay five to ten feet deep in the woods. The railroad was unable to operate and the twitch horses were starving in the logging camps, living off bark and harness leather, cribbing their stalls. The felled trees had disappeared under the snow and the Captain, who was on the Elk estimating the last timber on a twenty-thousand-acre tract, had to give up and return to the home place, breaking path all the way.

The Captain was ninety-one years old and his skin was the color of marble stone. What little was exposed to the wind and cold he'd covered with a layer of petroleum jelly. He traced his path back home, keeping on for a day and a night, his snowshoes silently lifting and falling, his cruising stick clasped in his mittened hand, because he knew to stop would be to stop forever.

When he returned, his daughter Clemmie was in the kitchen, in a rocking chair by the open fire. Her son, Henry, sat on the floor by her side, cross-legged on the wide stone hearth staring into the flames, his attention held by the sight of them and their oceanic noise.

She indicated that Henry should fetch more wood and so he stood, unfolding his body to its early awkward height. But he lingered in the doorway, half hidden by the jamb and listened.

"I must go," Clemmie said to her father, "and you cannot stop me."

"I know," he said.

The Captain made no argument but looked to the window and through to the darkness beyond. Of all his children, as many as three wives could give him, Clemmie was the youngest, the one who knew him best and she would be the first to ever leave him in this way. The rest had married away from him or fled the mountain without confrontation.

"Daddy," she said. "I cannot wait until you die. I can wait until spring," she said, relenting a bit, "but I must go."

Henry could read the Captain's face for his thinking: he had reconciled himself to the inevitability of Clemmie's leaving, but in waiting until spring, she would deny him the great impossible travel through the black and frozen land.

At melt time, the Captain escorted them down the miles of the Copperhead Road, some of the last land still treed, unmined, and inviolate.

They rode silently, on the backs of the offsprung generations of the coal black horses his grandfather loved so much. They rode down the rough track on the bloodlines of warriors, Clemmie riding behind her father and Henry following. They left behind the great looming house where she'd been born and he was born and the land where the Captain had been born. Henry looked back a last time and the house seemed to rise and climb the mountain. Still to see were the hanging terraces and curved steps, wet and gray and shining in the vitreous spring light.

In switchback turns they made their descent, in the cold perfume of the forest, the white pine, the laurel and dogwood understory, and he could feel in his chest an ache for the increasing density of the air as they descended.

Below them, a rising white torrent of runoff smashed through heads of stone. It suddenly disappeared inside the earth and then was with them again as they traveled its course. Clemmie and the Captain rode in silence, neither of them wanting to confront the confusion of their lives and the long histories that Henry did not understand. But he knew some of it, and it had to do with him and his mother's weariness and she not married and the father he did not know. There were whole days she'd be lost to him, turned inward and silent, and then other days she could not contain her restlessness.

If they could have, they would have ridden forever, as if riding were their calling, as if they were pilgrims with their holy land always a little farther along the path. They wanted and needed no accounting, as long as there was a length of trail ahead of them and no parting at the end.

The Captain asked Clemmie if she was ever in the city for he could not recall a time when she was.

"Yes," she said. "One time."

They were stopped to let the horses blow. All about was

the sound of a hollow wind running the land, but it was not the wind. It was the sound of the thaw, as what grew on the earth and clutched to the rock gave up the cold in an aching perceptible gasp.

"No," Clemmie said, reconsidering. "I guess I never was. I guess I just took that I was."

Her horse scuffed at the cobbled trail. Though noon, it was now dark again as if early in the morning and would be light for all but another few hours of the day as the cut where they stood was so deep and precipitous.

"Wherever you are, you will always think of me," the Captain said to Henry, his voice seeming to break with regret.

The trail became a road rutted with threadlike rivulets and late that day they came to the swollen Twelve Mile. They would have to make a dangerous crossing on a rickety footbridge and the Captain seemed to hesitate, but then he did not. Fog enveloped their path and Clemmie commented on how strange it was, the cold and wet about her legs and ankles, while her upper body was warming to the light.

The Captain held the reins of the coal black horses as they unlashed their bundles and shouldered them. First Clemmie and then Henry embraced the old man and then they turned and made their crossing over the swaying bridge that would soon be washed away with the melt.

"Don't look down," she said, as if it were something she'd heard and now was telling him.

When they reached the other side, Henry looked back. The Captain was still there, astride a coal black horse, the other two in hand. He raised his other hand, stretching forward his arm. Henry made the slightest of gestures, a nod in the Captain's direction, and the Captain stood in his stirrups, his old body arched in fierce salute.

THEY WENT TO LIVE in the city and Clemmie took a job working at the veterans' hospital where they got their cast-off towels and bedding and soap. She also saved for Henry the newspapers and magazines and books that were left behind.

It was near impossible to imagine not being in the mountains, but in the city the earth became the land at Henry's feet. To the west he could see what lay between himself and the horizon and it was without hollow, valley, defile, ravine, or stony turret. The mountains were never far away, but the site of the city was like something made by an originator, the mountains seemingly split open and pushed back by hand and then coved and held in place. He'd never walked so far in a straight flat line and felt turned out and naked.

Clemmie fell from a station in life she'd not known she occupied. Never before did they have to pay for water, heat, and a roof. They had a small house with a sun-filled kitchen and the hospital had a cafeteria where they often took their meals. On Saturday mornings Henry would go to the library with his mother. They'd walk through the back streets where clothes were hung on the lines to dry. The clothes wore a yellow hue from the burning of coal and they'd go to the library so he might pore over maps, atlases, and books of natural history, as if assuaging the privations of childhood. Then in the afternoon they'd purchase Italian ice sodas, almond, orange, or banana with shaved ice in tall, cloudy glasses. In the evenings Clemmie went to school and in time she became a nurse.

Sometimes they had visitors, relatives he'd never met before who'd been shunned by the Captain for having given themselves over to the life of the wage earner in the coal mines.

These relatives now lived in the city, or passed through, returning whenever they could. Uncle Golden came through when he was flush with money, and Aunt Adelita stayed with them for a time after her husband and two sons died in the Bartley No. 1 shaft mine. Ninety-one men and boys died that day, killed by explosion and fire, and his mother told him Aunt Adelita had been one of God's wandering souls ever since.

Aunt Adelita had unruly black hair she wore tied off in a ponytail. She cooked pot roast and mashed potatoes with string bean salad and bowls of chopped-up lettuce, and for dessert there'd be strawberry rhubarb pies or pineapple pies with blue cheese. It was as if she could not cook enough food to satisfy herself.

There were so many women, aunts and great-aunts, who'd buried husbands, dead from the wars, dead from the trauma of accidents — the celerity of white pine turned and twisted, split and shattered and descending from the sky, or under the earth where the kettlebottoms, petrified tree stumps, dropped from the roofs of mines to break a shoulder or stave in a skull. The women watched their children be hobbled by rickets, go deaf from untreated ear infections. They knew what it was to live on corn bread, molasses, and scrap and see their children eating dirt for the mineral it contained, and after a time they turned a bend in life and their teeth went bad, their lovely strong backs and shoulders grew humped and stooped, their knuckles thickened from chores and cold, and their cheeks and necks grew hollow.

The men in Henry's family, they were big, sprawling, raw boned. They were angular, muscular, warlike and discontented. They farmed and mined and logged and framed out houses and worked the shipyards, and they quarreled beyond reconciliation and then it would be forgotten. From them Henry learned the stories of his grandfather and his old uncles. He learned that if any one of them was threatened they would descend with all stealth and fury, with gun or knife or torch or dynamite. They were a family relentless in their hatreds.

It was in one of those newspapers where they read that Uncle Golden died by his own hand after an eight-hour standoff along the highway. There'd been a high-speed chase, reaching ninety miles an hour, until finally he lost control and went off the road. He lay in the wreck the whole time threatening to shoot anyone who came near and finally put the gun to his own head. In the newspaper, it never said why.

But for the most, they were homesick castaway men who worked in the shipyards in Norfolk, men who built the Golden Gate Bridge, Boulder Dam, the Holland Tunnel. They smoked Lucky Strike and Camel cigarettes and carried them rolled in the sleeves of their T-shirts. They drove old Pontiacs that chugged exhaust fumes and they moved as tender and wary animals. They were polite and solicitous of Clemmie. They'd ask her of the Captain as if they were supplicants and she the last of the blessed, and as the years passed and as Henry grew older, one by one, they disappeared.

Chapter 2

THE CINNAMON BAY NAMED Gaylen was the sweetest horse Henry ever knew. She was not standoffish but always interested in him and what he was about and would walk right up to him to see what he was doing. Walter said she was a peach and a natural beauty. He called her a poetic horse.

Walter was a horseman and veteran of the first war and owned the stables across the river. Walter knew Henry's mother from the veterans' hospital where they worked on his legs. One day he mentioned that he needed a hired hand and the next day Henry rode his bicycle across the river and up the mountain and asked him for the job. That was three years ago when the Gaylen horse first arrived.

The stables weren't much. They were rundown and ramshackle and by then there were few who paid to ride or take lessons or board their horses. The horses were grades of indeterminate parentage and small and heavily muscled cobs with strong bones and steady dispositions that the children liked to ride. They were all easy keepers and constituted with a steady temperament, strength, and stamina and no great turn of speed. They liked to be with each other and when they were in the barn they needed to see each other between the stalls. They tolerated well each other's personalities, faults, and vices.

But Gaylen was different. She came from up north. She stood fifteen hands and was light and muscular, well knit with flat-boned legs, laid-back shoulders, a deep and compact body that was smooth over the top line and into the croup. She had a nice length of neck and clean-cut throatlatch. Her eyes were large and revealing. The Gaylen horse was a free-going, graceful, enduring traveler and Walter claimed he'd been offered ten times over what he paid for her, but no matter what, he wouldn't sell her.

The Gaylen horse was favored by Mercy, a senior in high school. Henry was a junior that spring of 1950 and he did not know Mercy before she started riding at the stables because she went to a private academy for girls. Her father was a judge known for the empery of his opinions, his craggy face, his low bulging forehead, gold incisor, and wealth. Mercy seemed not to have a mother as she never made mention of her.

The stables were prettiest in the spring and summer when the flowers bloomed in long thin beds of loam and dried horse manure. There were tended ranks of tulips and daffodils and in the summer came huddles of stalky gladiolas. Snowball bushes with masses of blossoms in white, pink, and lavender and lilacs and dogwood and rose-bays fixed the corners. There were hives where Walter kept bees that made a floral honey he sold by the jar. There were times Walter reminded Henry of his grandfather and the stables the home place.

Henry had worked into the night and had school in the

morning and was waiting for Walter to return from a mysterious appointment.

But he was not eager to get home. Three days ago word had come that his grandfather died and each night thereafter Clemmie had fallen into an uneasy sleep: waking, starting, sleeping again, her grief so consuming. She did not so much live within her being but occupied it the way one holds to a strange land with unpredictable weather.

He grieved for the old man too. The Captain was the only father he'd ever known, and though he sometimes wondered about his own father it was hard to miss something he'd never had.

Last night in his sleep he sensed she was awake and so he woke too. It was raining outside and on his ceiling was the watery play of the streetlights. She told him she was hot and asked for water. He poured a glass from the pitcher. He opened the window and fetched a damp cloth to cool her forehead.

"No rest for the wicked," she sighed, holding his hand.

"You are not wicked," he said.

"I dreamt it was winter and snowing. Bitter cold."

"It will be soon enough again."

"I am so sad," she said.

He took her into his arms and held her against his chest.

"Is it horrible of me to be relieved?" she asked, and he assured her that it was not.

She stared at him and he didn't know what to do. He could not console her. She bit at the damp cloth and held it in her teeth. She turned her face and began to weep again.

"Something is going to happen," she said.

"What?"

"I don't know," she said. "But whatever it is, it isn't going to be good."

He could not penetrate the strange wildness of her expression. Her world was too complex, bewildering: the attacks of loneliness, the black dogs of her twitching sleep, her sleep-walking. There were moments when she seemed to have lost all touch with the earth and she'd just sit, her dark-ringed eyes staring at nothing, not speaking.

He knew enough of the past to know how it could haunt a being, and as much as it was grief it seemed to be that kind of pain as well: dim, historical, and universal. His mother cared about sin. She cared about the long dead and prayed for their well-being though seldom inside the walls of a church. She cared about the poor and the hungry and was fond of giving away whatever she had to give. Of late, their little house in the city had taken on the austerity of a nunnery.

"Something bad?" he said, but she had no more to say, and however discontent her sleep might be, each morning she inhabited her kitchen with a strange radiance and the next morning was no different.

"You have always been such a good boy," she said, thanking him for his care and tenderness. She was cooking his breakfast and packing their lunches and told him how much she loved him and wanted to know about his life.

"There's nothing to tell," he said.

"You have a sweetheart yet?"

"No, nothing like that."

"You will," she said, and told him someday he would leave her for someone else and when that happened it would be okay.

"I worry about you," he said.

"It doesn't happen all at once," she said, and smiled. "You lose your mind in stages. I will be okay."

THE RAIN WAS letting up. He drew deeply on his cigarette. He tried to make sense of the indecipherable. He did not know if he understood love. He knew he loved his mother and she loved him, but he did not understand if he could love someone else or not.

Drops of water continued to fall from the eaves of the low-spreading roof. He fingered a frayed buttonhole as he stared off into the pines. He thought of his grandfather. Death was not difficult to understand. You were alive and then you were not.

He felt the eyes of the Gaylen horse on his back. He finished his smoke and pinched it off. When he turned to her she nickered and stretched toward him. In the damp light-less barn he let her nuzzle his open coat until she found the licorice he carried. He lifted the flap on his breast pocket to reveal the sticks and the horse ate them as if eating from his chest. She blew gently and nosed his chest and then she let her chin rest on his shoulder.

"Easy as pie," he said, his face to her cheek, and told her it was time for him to get going.

He pulled up his collar and stepped into the wet haze. He could see the lights in the city below and the lights on the river, sparkling like wire-strung jewels, the boats and barges and all the little boathouses. There was a flowery smell in the air, strange and sourceless, and from the stables the occasional tromp of slow bodies shifting hooves. He thought it would be a pretty night with the stars coming on.

Somebody was calling his name. Walter helloed again, slammed the door to his truck and leaned against it.

"What's the good news?" Henry called out.

"There's a devil on my shoulder whispering in my ear."

"What's he sayin'?"

"Life's a game and it's rigged. What's your story?"

"I ain't got one."

"Dirty weather," Walter said grimly when Henry came up. "Ain't good for bid'ness. Keeps the money away."

"That all he says?"

"That's enough."

Walter's face was pale white and his lips were shaded blue. He had the arthritis bad and a twitchy airway. His respiration was slow and irregular. He quietly gasped when he breathed and conversation was difficult for him. Always about him was the smell of mentholatum.

"Chores done?"

"Yessir," Henry said.

"Come in for coffee?" Walter said.

"No thanks."

"I was going to have some for myself and I am asking you if you'd like some."

Henry followed Walter inside to the tack room where he'd cut a door into the adjacent stall and fashioned a two-room apartment. He had a hot plate, kerosene heater, an icebox, and he'd installed a Murphy bed. He walked painfully, each step a decision. During the early days of the first war his unit was bombed and his knee shattered and he'd been shot in the eye. There were pink scars on his cheeks and he had medals he kept in a cigar box. The one eye was now glass and his good eye turned inward toward his nose.

"What's for dinner?" Henry said.

"Oh, I'll stodge up something," Walter said.

The windows were open, but the damp shut out the air and the room smelled of the barn: hay, manure, sweat, leather, and oats.

"How's your mother?" Walter said.

"She's good."

Most days Walter wore overalls and a blue and gold Legion cap, but today he was hatless, his skull bald and gaunt, and he wore creased khakis, a pressed blue chambray shirt, and tennis shoes.

"She is good," Walter declared. "She is an angel walking the ground. I gave up women years ago, but she's a good one."

"How do you know she's good?"

"I seen her today."

"Where'd you see her?"

"Down at the VA. She looked good."

Walter set out two mugs. He splashed rye whisky into his and held up the bottle. His good eye wet and glittering. Henry shrugged and Walter splashed some in his mug too and then he filled both mugs with coffee from a vacuum bottle.

"The main thing is to keep a woman busy," Walter said.

Walter carried his mug to a splintered sideboard where he fixed a plate of ham, boiled eggs, bread, and butter.

"Baseball starts soon," Walter said.

Henry held up his hands, his fingers spread.

"Ten day," Walter said, tossing him an egg.

"Ten," Henry said, catching the egg.

They drank quietly, Henry waiting patiently for what Walter had to say. He knew there was no point in hurrying him. He worked his thumb inside the eggshell and peeled it away.

At last Walter said, "I have to go into hospital. They are going to take care of this leg and tuther one."

Henry's first thought was the horses, their feed, water, and care, and whatever small business there was, who would conduct it.

"I have been praying for a long time it wouldn't come to this."

"What about the bid'ness?" Henry said.

"The bid'ness is not lost on me."

"I can stay here."

"That's what I'm wantin' to ask you," Walter said.

"I can do that."

"What about school and baseball and your good mother?"

"I will explain it to them."

"That would be a great service to me."

"When do you go?"

"Now," Walter said.

"You going to make it?"

"I am not about to lay down and die, if that's what you're asking."

Walter's powers of endurance seemed extraordinary. There were days he could not mount a horse because of the pain and once on he rarely dismounted for fear of not being able to step back into the stirrup.

"It was first the one," Walter said, "and now both knees burn like hell."

He never complained, but there were whole days his face was the tight mask of pain and the cast of his spirit one of torment and suffering.

"They say you use more butter when it's soft than when it's hard. How can that be?"

"I never thought about it," Henry said.

"What's yor' blood type?"

Henry shrugged.

"That's something you ought to know."

"What's yours?"

"I don't 'member," Walter said. He finished buttering a slice of bread and folded it in half. He worked up his quid of tobacco, spit it into his hand, and tossed it aside.

"Someday," Walter said, waving his fold of bread in the air, "there will be giant mechanical brains to cook and take dictation." With a flourish, he stuffed half the folded slice into his mouth, closed his eyes, and chewed.

"That will be something to see," Henry said.

"All my troubles," Walter said, "come from the fact that my 'magination is a little more active than those of others."

Walter pulled himself erect, and then hobbled over to a cupboard, its door hung with a cracked mirror. He paused and looked into the mirror.

"You look like shit," he said.

From the cupboard he removed a white glass jar and a pair of tweezers and returned to the table.

"I am afraid my life is vanishing," he said. "Do you ever feel that way?"

"No," Henry said. "Sometimes."

"I need a swallow of the strong," Walter said, and took another drink of the whisky and coffee he favored. He unbuckled his belt and let his khakis fall to the floor before sitting down. Then he loosed the bale on the white glass jar and slid open the top. He went inside with the tweezers and came out with a bee in their gentle pinch.

"How bad is it?" Henry said.

"What?"

"The pain."

"You won't know until it happens to you."

Walter held the bee's abdomen to his bony knee. His eye flashed brightly and his nostrils widened. "Oh," he said with each pull of the barb. "Oh." His face reddened, his leg shook, his forehead broke with sweat. "Oh," he said, releasing the bee. "Oh," he said, closing his eyes and letting his head go back.

After a brief time, he discarded the bee and went into the jar for another. He gritted his teeth and administered to his other knee, receiving the venom as if a secret current of life. His shoulders drooped and he breathed slowly, carefully.

They sat for another spell, the stables silent, Walter in his skivvies, his trousers stacked at his shoe tops and Henry straddling a chair.

When Walter looked up again his face was red and drenched with sweat and he was laughing.

"What's so funny?" Henry said.

"You know what they said? It is shrapnel rising to the surface. After all these years, little pieces less the size of needles floating around inside my legs."

Walter closed his eyes again. He swabbed at the wetness with his shirt cuff and breathed until the rasp in his throat softened.

He rested again and then he reached for his trousers pooled at his ankles and in a single motion he stood and pulled them up.

"You're not the kind to leave someone in the lurch," he said.

Walter nodded to the bottle and Henry poured him half a mug.

"Good idea," Walter said, and with trembling red fingers he lifted the mug and took a drink. He packed another chaw and fed it into his mouth.

"I will now see the Gaylen horse," Walter said.

Henry fetched the wheelbarrow. He tipped it forward and Walter settled into its barrel, his legs dangling over the front. Henry levered the handles and when he did he made a groaning sound.

"How much you weigh these days?" Henry said.

"A hunnerd and sixty pound."

"That all?" Henry said, wheeling him to the door.

"Not a ounce more."

"Then you must sit pretty heavy."

The sound of Walter's laughter, coarse and harsh, brought the horses from their feed and water. They stood at their stall doors where they curved their necks and shook their heads. They stepped in place, nickering and whinnying, anticipating Walter's arrival.

Chapter 3

THE GAYLEN HORSE MOVED up slope with increasing confidence and speed, exercising the strength in her hindquarters. Henry thought how when he reached ridgeline he could ride this horse from the face of the land and into the sky and to the sliver of the pale moon just hung.

The world was black and blue with the silver light of the stars come down to earth and silent except for the leather creak, the shake of the horse, the muffled rattle and stretch of tack, the lunging breaths, as they made the ridgeline and traversed the darkling landscape. There was the smell of pine and cold and horse and the wax smell of Henry's leather boots.

For three nights he'd ridden the horse on this mountain trail. They traveled to the edge of the forest, the swart green pines a wall into the night. Up here he felt by particle and thread the fluence that rode the cold air.

All day long he'd been at the stable when he should have been in school. The two-storied brick building was a place of half-rolled shades and smudged blackboards, the *Encyclopaedia Britannica* kept under lock and key. He actually liked school and he did well. He especially liked playing baseball, but knew he wouldn't be going back again. He knew it was just killing time until he'd be leaving for Chicago, Detroit, Gary: stockyards, car factories, steel mills.

He fished a Lucky Strike from his breast pocket. The cherry ember hissed and crackled. To the west were the distant tin-walled warehouses, the Union Carbide plant. On the wind came the sulfurous exhaust from the smelting furnaces and rolling mills. Mixed in the air it smelled like noxious violets and disappeared.

There was no spirit world that lived in the pitchy night, just him and this horse. And when morning came the ground fog burned slowly off the paddocks and leaf shade quaked on the ground. Then early that evening there was a moment before darkness when the sun became apparent and slanted rays hit his face. It was going to be another long night at the rundown stables above the river and he wished it would not end.

He'd parcel out the oats and flakes of hay. He'd water and then telephone his mother and then turn on the radio and listen to the baseball broadcast. He'd let himself imagine for the time these were his horses and this was his stable.

But he was not foolish.

It'll last as long as it lasts, he thought, and touched with his heels and pressed with his legs and Gaylen tossed her head and was spurred into flashy motion.

In chill and moonlight they returned to the stables. Parked in the yard was an automobile, the engine shut down, the glare of headlights still hung in the stirry mist. He tightened his legs on Gaylen's barrel as he crossed through the light and then dismounted. The low mist covered the ground and he could not see his feet. He walked Gaylen over to the automobile.

It was Mercy parked at the white-rail fence. She stood next to the automobile waiting for him. She wore her hair in a tight knot at the back of her head and a wide strawberry-colored scarf about her neck and shoulders. She carried her head on a tilt, her mouth like a soft flower. She stood with her hands on her hips as if she'd been waiting too long and he was late.

"Cut your lights," Henry said, "or you will empty your batt'ry."

"What's going on here?" she wanted to know.

"Not much."

"Where's Walter?"

"He is in the hospital recovering from an operation."

"Why didn't he tell me?"

"That's none of my business," Henry said, and turned on his heel and led Gaylen back through the paddock and through the wide door and into the long gallery of the board and batten barn. He cross-tied the horse and removed her saddle and fleece pad. Outside, the automobile engine dragged and started and roared. There was a sweep of head-lights and Mercy was gone.

He put his face to Gaylen's coat and let his weight lean into her side. He did not want to let go her infinite sweetness. He bathed the horse with warm water and toweled her dry. He shook out hay and then in the tack room he pulled off his boots and took off his jacket and shirt and lay down.

The next day after school, Mercy returned again. She

brought a can of coffee and a sack of crullers. She had apples for the horses. In a sack she handed him there was hard candy and he took one and slipped it into his mouth. As he went back to his chores, she groomed and saddled and haltered Gaylen and then led her into the ring.

Henry tied a red bandanna across his forehead and over that he wore a broad straw hat. He left off his chores to stand at the rail in the late sunlight.

"It's quite a good day," she called out, and he nodded in agreement.

Gaylen was mesmerizing to watch. She was a forward-moving animal with an elliptical stride, picking up her feet and reaching for distance with the action of her knee, but nobody rode her like Mercy. She was a pretty rider, consonant with the horse's every motion.

Henry ducked between the rails and moved to the center. He turned in place while the horse and rider made their revolutions. Mercy's hands were quiet and held close to the neck, her legs resting along the horse's sides and held still. She looked up and ahead. Then he spoke.

"I want you to take a holt of your reins and push up into the bridle with your legs."

Mercy did as he suggested. Gaylen's head set and stayed as if in a frame, both horse and rider looking up and ahead.

Henry stepped from the center and walked a smaller circle beside them.

"Keep her moving along at a brisk trot," he said, and then, "Lift your hand a little so that she keeps her head up. You don't want her head so low."

Mercy lifted her hands. She held her shoulders back, her elbows bent at her sides and the line from her shoulder through her elbow, hip and ankle was straight as an arrow.

"Canter," Henry said.

Mercy pressed the horse into canter and the horse joyfully stepped into the three-beat gait. Mercy sat back in her saddle, keeping the horse slow and steady, keeping her in frame.

"Keep her light. Keep your leg on her," Henry said. "Don't let her pull the reins out of your hands."

Mercy and Gaylen circled him in harmony, light and cadenced as if made for each other.

She returned every day that week. On Friday she stayed and helped him finish up with his chores and afterward they made coffee and ate the sugary crullers she brought and took their coffee outside to drink, the mugs warming their hands. Some distance from the stables he sat down on the ground and she sat beside him.

"Want a smoke?" he asked, but she declined and then neither of them spoke or moved.

"I've not been here at night so late before," she said. "It is so quiet. You must sleep well."

"Quietness scares away sleep," he said, feeling foolish for the pith of such a comment.

"I won't quarrel with that," she said.

Moonlight shone on them, cast through the trees and thin as glassy water. He fought how suddenly aware he was of her presence.

"My father says I should ride at the new stable."

"Why don't you?" he said, though it hurt a little to say.

"He says if I do he'll buy me a horse."

"Sounds like a good deal."

"He tried to buy Gaylen, but Walter said she wasn't for sale."

His blood slowed. He'd not known her father tried to buy Gaylen. Why should he know? He was just a hired man.

"There's a lot of other horses for sale."

"But I don't want a horse."

"Every girl wants a horse."

"I am not every girl."

There came the plangent call of a whippoorwill deep in the forest and they listened to its cry. He whistled up its call and he went back and forth with the bird for the longest time.

"What do you do with yourself?" he said. "When you're not riding."

"I study a lot. What about you?"

"I like to play baseball."

"They say you are very good."

"Who says that?"

"People."

Her blue eyes held a certain transparency and at times were passionate and at other times becalmed, but rarely were they at peace. She was wearing blue jeans and a red wool sweater and smelled of hand soap. Her abundant hair was combed exactly down the middle and tied back.

"What about you?" he said. He was asking questions purely for the sake of it.

"I am going to the university in the fall."

He was suddenly aware in his flannel shirt of the smell

of old sweat. His chest tightened and he squinted his eyes. Beyond the mountain there was no light and was as if the bottom of darkness.

"Can you feel that?" she said.

"What?"

"I am touching your shadow."

"My shadow," he said, turning quickly as if to catch a glimpse of fleeting presence.

"Your moon shadow."

He made a sound and then he lit another cigarette. He wanted her to leave and go home and be left alone. Their worlds were too different and he barely understood his own.

"Well, you get some sleep," she said. "I will come back tomorrow."

She stood and brushed off the seat of her blue jeans. The moon's light was cutting a silvery path in the night down to the ground. She plucked a piece of straw from his flannel shirt and held it in her teeth. She was smiling with the play of her private thoughts before she spoke.

"When I leave, will you remember me?" she asked.

"Do you want me to?"

"Yes," she said.

"Then I will."

He watched her moving figure. She was walking away into what seemed an empty world, the silver stripped trees like skeletons. He could hear the engine and saw a sweep of light and she was gone.

Chapter 4

EACH DAY HE BECAME more and more aware of Mercy's lovely face looking at him, her chestnut hair tied loosely beneath a scarf, her fragile blue eyes. Each day she seemed closer than the day before and each day he busied himself even more and tried to keep his distance, but nights she would find him and she would bring groceries and they would talk and they would share coffee and food.

While she rode he hurried to finish his chores and made coffee and took it outside to a nearby picnic table.

When she joined him she'd untied her hair. She sat down beside him and stretched and yawned.

"It's a fine night," she said.

"Yes, it is," he said. They'd been eating together for how many nights now, he could not remember. Maybe six. Maybe seven. He tried to remember, but his mind fell away with the blended memories of each night's events.

"Can I get you anything?" he said.

"Nothing. I came to keep you company," she said, and sipped at her coffee.

"I appreciate it," Henry said, and offered her a cigarette, which she always declined.

There was the rising of damp and the falling of cold. Their breath hung in the air under the dark spring sky. It was a silent night, the horses quiet and sleepy.

"It's beautiful," she said, looking into the sky. Her face was soft, almost childlike, and seemed almost in a trance of delight. She turned to him.

"You've got the handsomest face," Mercy said. She leaned into him, jostled him, and smiled. When she smiled her eyes narrowed and the light inside them was condensed.

He thanked her and told her she was the prettiest girl.

"You probably think that's dumb," she said.

"No. I don't think that's dumb at all."

"All the time you rise up as if to say something and then you don't say anything."

"I only wish I could have met you better in life," Henry said.

"Better than what?" she said, and slung an arm across his shoulders.

He lifted his hand and made a dismissive gesture. How could he reply to that? He stood and stepped away, his hands behind his back, one hand holding the wrist of the other.

"What are you thinking?" Mercy said.

He told her he dreamt of her last night.

"I dreamt of you last night too," she said.

Mercy went to him and reached her hand to his cheek. She ran her fingers down the side of his face. She told him the spots he must've missed when he shaved that morning. It seemed to take a long time. Her body was soft and close. She took him by his shirt front to hold him. He began to laugh. A mass of disheveled hair surrounded her face.

"Are you in there?" he asked, sorting through her hair to her face with his fingers.

"I am right here," she said, and he took her in his arms and held her.

This moment was enough forever and he wanted time to stop. Overhead was the twining of the stars and stars caught in the tops of the pine trees. The smell of her hair. The air so thick and heavy. She was entirely herself, her hair around her face and at the back of her neck. He almost could not breathe. She stroked his hair and for some reason she began to cry and he kissed away her wet salty eyes.

She took a deep breath as if preparing to go still deeper. She said, her voice barely audible, "All my life I have been strong, but now it is a hard thing to do."

She stepped back and looked down at the ground.

"Don't be shy," she said, as if talking to herself, and stepped forward and took his face in her hands. She closed her eyes and then she kissed him and she left.

Sometime in the night he awoke. He left the bed and pulled a chair to the window where he sat and looked out. A star fell from the sky, hot and streaking and without reason. The place he was in was somewhere he did not know and where he had never been before, somewhere on the earth and under the sky. It was nighttime. Or earliest morning. He did not know.

From the long galley there came a nickering sound. Gaylen.

He believed he heard footsteps coming to his door. He hoped it was she and when the door swung dim light into the room he could see that it was. He reached to light a bulb for them to see by. Her hair was a braid she wore wrapped twice around her head. She was cold and held her arms clasped to her chest.

The watery light pressed against the cold in the room. She was shivering. He crossed the room to start the little kerosene heater.

"You are a thief," she said.

"Why am I a thief?"

"You stole my heart."

"I didn't steal anything," Henry said.

"I want you," she said.

"How much do you want?"

"How much do I want? I want everything you have."

"I don't have anything," he said.

"Maybe you will have to learn to see yourself in a different way," Mercy said.

"Maybe we will both need to see ourselves differently."

She unbuttoned her riding pants and slid them down over her hips. The room was cold with night and she shivered again as she pulled off her sweater.

He threw back the blanket, and she let her body, light and smooth skinned, as if she were the petals of a rose, lay down in the warmth he'd left behind. He slid in beside her and took her in his arms. He liked how dense and thick and well muscled her thighs and hips were from so much riding.

"Tell me about the girls you have been with. Who were they and what were they like?"

"I've never been with anyone," he said.

"Me neither," she said.

Her skin smelled of nutmeg and clove. His hands fit her ribs and he could hold her ass in his open palms. At first he shied from her mouth and then she was insistent. She found his mouth and that first night was his hands and his mouth and their bodies.

As he hovered over her, she held him by his elbows and she told him she felt her body dividing. She closed on him and kept him inside her and bit his shoulder.

"Don't move," she said, and he answered her by not moving and then she splayed her legs and there were contractions deep inside her and she gasped. She folded herself around him again and held him inside her and she would not let him go.

When he came it was as if a violence inside his body. His legs shook and his arms quivered.

She had wanted it and he had wanted it too. She said she hoped for it to happen and then she said she prayed for it to happen. She said it was what she wanted even more than she wanted him. But he did not mind.

Then she told him he could move and he rolled to his side. She stared up at the rafters and told him she loved him, and when he told her he loved her too she told him he didn't have to tell her that.

"Not even if I want to?" he said.

"If you want to, you can," she said.

Outside the window was north and the stars and the cold river.

"Will you always love me?" Mercy said.

"Always," he said.

"No matter what?"

"No matter what."

He held her in his arms and sometime after, while she slept, he slipped from the bed and across the room he found the water pitcher and drank from it. He shivered in his nakedness. He was still wet with their lovemaking. That's how soon she'd fallen asleep and how soon he left the warm bed. He could not imagine being so far away from her and went back and pulled up a chair beside the bed. He thought to sleep but never wanted to sleep again.

She turned in her sleep. He wondered what she was dreaming. Her dream seemed intense and possessive. He thought to hear his name, but it was only a sound she made. She turned again in the bed. He reached to touch her, to assure her of his presence, but she startled and turned away from his touch.

"Is everything all right," she asked suddenly, sitting up in the bed.

"I feel like you took my spine," Henry said, and smiled.

"Your spine," she said, as if she'd finally captured the prize.

"Sleep some more," he said.

"I think it's the best thing," she said, and drew him into the bed and turned the side of her face to his chest and was asleep again.

He thought about their lovemaking and how it had been like speaking to each other. Their lovemaking was like finding the only other person on earth who spoke the same words in the same way you did.

A bird had awakened and was beginning its morning song.

It was that close to sunrise. He thought how he loved her and how he had never loved a girl before. Or perhaps he had never loved at all. It could have been that, though he knew he loved his mother.

He smiled at how strange his thoughts.

It was cold in the room. It was the cold the sun pushes in its distant rising. The bird went silent. Henry lifted from the bed and as quietly as possible he dressed, pulled on his ball cap and went outside. In the east was a kindling of pale rose and silver that lengthened and brightened along the horizon. A garland of mist roped through the crowns.

He thought maybe he'd not wanted to confront the death of his grandfather until this very morning and now he could think of nothing else. But how could that be? His chest ached and his face burned. He thought how shallow his history and yet how complex the threads of memory. He never once thought he'd die and thought there was all the time in the world and he'd see him again. He wanted a home feeling, but he just couldn't find it.

He heard Mercy before he saw her. Her hair was combed exactly down the middle and tied. She knelt beside him. She picked up a stick and scratched at the ground. Down the valley was the sun-glittering edge of the water, its dark green sluggish flow, the placid stretches, its darkling pools.

"What are you doing?" she said.

"Thinking."

"About what?"

"Did you ever think about the rocks?" he said.

"How does that one go?"

"Maybe they are alive and their hearts beat once every thousand years and they only need to take a breath every five hundred."

"You shouldn't feel so alone again," she said.

The brassy light hit her and her skin soon mottled from how intense the sunlight. She pulled on his ball cap and adjusted her collar. She found her gloves in her back pocket and tucked her hands inside them. Then she tugged at his sleeve and told him she'd started breakfast.

When they went in she had for him bread, milk, bacon, coffee, and eggs. And then she worked away with a mop and a bucket until the room was clean smelling.

Chapter 5

That spring, for Mercy's graduation, Henry wore a dark suit, a starched white shirt, and a red tie. He wore new shoes and they were stiff and still wore a store shine. That night there was a dinner dance at the country club for the graduates whose families were members.

She had a brand-new Mercury convertible she received as a graduation present. It was maroon with a white leather interior and that night when she picked him up she brought for him a gray flannel suit. She wore bare touches of rouge and lipstick and a strand of white pearls. She kissed him on the cheek and laughed and wiped away the kiss mark. She was going to the university in the fall and he still had another year of high school, but it did not matter to them. She'd have her own automobile and they would see each other often.

"But I can't take that," he said, dry mouthed and light headed.

"You have to know how to take," she said, and smiled and passed the new suit into his hands and then she kissed him again.

At the country club, the lights changed from orange to

red to yellow, and paper trees swayed gently all in the same direction as if leaned by an invisible wind.

Mercy's father was there and her brother, Randall. Randall was a lawyer and married and had a family and was there with his wife. Randall was tall like his father and both men wore white linen suits and silk bow ties. They smoked cigars and held glasses of bourbon and were surrounded by men much like themselves.

When Mercy introduced Henry they were polite and firmly shook his hand. Randall's wife, Beverly, was delighted to finally meet him. She'd heard so much.

A man in a black tuxedo with satin piping sang into a microphone. He was slender and had a pencil-thin mustache, slicked-back and shiny black hair. His voice was soothing and seemed more an instrument of music than a voice. He held a gourd in each hand and when he shook them the sound was like water on the shore. Henry and Mercy danced, but they did not really dance. It was more the shape of dancing and the gesture of dancing as they slowly moved across the floor. Henry's sleeve caught a glass and it tumbled to the floor and smashed, and everyone cheered. On the lawn, under the spangled sky, they played a game of croquet with an older couple she knew and who called him young man.

A storm had been threatening all that day and it exploded and the power went out and for the time he lost her in the darkness and did not find her again until the lights came back on. After the dance she handed him the keys to the Mercury. She was upset and would not tell him why. He started the engine and the dashboard lit up and glowed. He cut on the lights and shined the river.

"Just drive," she said.

"Where are we going?"

"Go," she said, and after waiting for him to make a move, she said it again. "Go."

They left the city and climbed into the mountains. They drove the long balconies of stone, a world extant from the world of the street, a world womblike in its whispery green luxuriance. The world up there was newly wet and cooler by degrees, cooler than the street world. The rooms of the forest were deep and cathedral and what rose to them was scent and closeness, and nothing could be heard but the gently soughing wind.

He told her he was looking for her when the lights went out and was afraid he'd lost her. She hiked up her skirt and crossed her leg over his.

"Do you want some of this?" Mercy said.

She folded closer and he kissed her ear and her neck as he drove. She unknotted his tie and unbuttoned his shirt enough to drag it off his shoulder and lay her face against his chest. She took his hand and held it between her legs.

He was in a world where his ascension was never lost to him. It was a world where she would always want him between her legs. She would bite down hard on the muscle that strapped his shoulder cuff, the insides of her strong legs, her fingers in his mouth, the runnels of sweat streaking his back and pooling in the skin of her sunken belly. Her fingers bruising his skin. The fury and the rush of their pumping blood.

Henry knew he would never forget her if it ever ended. He did not know why, but this night he had the sad feeling it would never again in his life be this way.

At four in the morning they drove the dark streets to his house and when she dropped him off she pulled away slowly and he walked along with her, his arms still resting on the window. She stopped to kiss him one more time. She told him if he ever lost her again he could find her at the boathouse.

"Remember that," she said. "Tell me you will."

"I will," he said.

"Do you love me?" she said.

"Don't you know?" he said, and she smiled.

"I will see you later," she said, and drove away.

He slept for a few hours and when he awoke it was to the scent of lilacs in the air. He could feel spring's ascending light, its joyful degrees of increasing brightness. But the winter had held deep into the spring with the days still cold and dark and the nights requiring sweaters and a blanket.

He awoke to spring that morning, or turned around or blinked an eye, and it was as if those days of cold never were.

His head throbbed from so much drink. The champagne and the gin and then more champagne. The flannel suit lay draped on the chair and the room seemed particularly sad and desolate as if from an event canceled. He wiped at his face and Mercy was still on his hands, her faint scent, the trail of her perfume still on his skin. The night he remembered verged on the improbable and he wondered if it ever really happened at all.

That afternoon, the sun a perfect white disk in the sky, she

did not come to the game as promised. Parked at the edge of
the ball field was a black Oldsmobile and it was there for the
length of the game. When he walked home the Oldsmobile
pulled up beside him, the tar bubbles popping beneath the
tread of its tires. It pulled ahead and then pulled over beside
the road. He came alongside it and the window went down
and he saw it was Mercy's father sitting in the driver's seat.
Her father looked at him and raised his finger.

"You're a real good ballplayer," he said, letting his finger
down.

"Thank you, sir."

Mercy's father unwrapped a cigar. He looked at it and set
it in his mouth. He struck a stick match with his thumb-
nail and held it while it burned and then dropped it out the
window. If he had intention of smoking the cigar, he made
no further effort to light it. He turned his attention back to
Henry.

"It's over now, son. You go back to your people."

Henry's cheeks began to burn like hot brass as he understood his embarrassment and humiliation. He understood
the disparity between her family and his, but his mind could
not accept it. Shame washed through him, a boy's shame
burning like acid.

Mercy's father held the gaze, secure in the dominion of
self. Henry could not endure the man's stare and had to look
down. His hand dropped into his pocket. He felt the blunt-
ness of unbelievable anguish. He was still a boy. He shuffled
his feet. He knew it was not in his nature to live as one who
feared. He let the baseball bat slip off his shoulder, and when

he did, the passenger door of the black Oldsmobile flew open and Randall stepped out. Randall'd been an athlete himself and still moved with an athlete's strength and ease. Henry had the sense there was someone else in the backseat, but he could not see who it was.

Randall stepped up to him and took his measure. He kicked away the bat and knocked off Henry's ball cap. Randall made to step into him, but Mercy's father stayed him with a raised hand and said for him to get back in the car and he obeyed.

"It will never be," her father said, as if his words were fashioned from a god arrogant and enduring. He then rolled up his window and drove away.

Henry felt anger and hatred and then he just felt hatred.

Chapter 6

THE COLORS OF THE day faded in the east while to the west they still flared in an angry burl of violet, reds, and deepening blue ash. In the kitchen there was coffee and butter cakes with a compote of wet cherries.

The hours ticked by as he sat at the kitchen table, still wearing his baseball uniform, shuffling again a deck of dog-eared cards. He dealt out another hand of solitaire. He scrutinized the tableau before him. He rubbed the stock deck with his thumb, but he did not play. He tried to remember: how many meaningless games, how many hours of killed time? Inside he remained kindled from the day's confrontation and could not escape the burning smell in his nostrils, like the sulfur smell that comes from gunpowder.

Clemmie came down the stairs and into the kitchen. She wore her bathrobe and slippers and her hair tied back with an elastic. She'd worked a double shift at the VA and went up to bed after dinner and should have been sleeping, but she could not and was wandering the house.

"You're still up," she said, yet half awake, touching at her eyes with her fingertips.

"What about you?" he said.

"I can't sleep," she said, and waved her hand, such a bother.

At the sink she filled a glass and drank half. The pipes banged and echoed from beneath the house. She looked at the glass and then drank the rest.

"Why can't you sleep?" Henry said.

"I had a bad dream," she said. "I cannot seem to relieve my mind."

She took his hand and pressed it to her chest. Outside the flying insects tapped at the window glass.

"Your heart's beating so fast," he said, and turned in his chair.

"I don't remember most of it, but I can't forget all of it," she said. "Not the feel of it, not the worst."

"Do you want to tell me about it?"

"I feel like I have heavy stones in the pit of my stomach," she said. "But talking about some things is worse than not talking about them."

"But there's something I want to say."

"Go ahead," she said, her hand at his face. "You can tell me whatever you want."

"I am thinking of going away," Henry said. He could see the sudden fright his words made in his mother's face.

"You can't," she said, catching herself. "What about the team and your man Walter? He depends on you. Where would you go?"

"I don't know. I haven't made up my mind," Henry said. He wanted to call back the words he'd spoken.

"What a funny thought — making up your mind. Like a bed or a story."

Then her eyes seemed to gaze from a place far beyond the walls of their little house. She squeezed his hand.

"You are really leaving," she said. There was a resignation in her voice and it was then she must have seen how shattered he was, how great the disquiet that possessed him. She took his face in her hands that she might see the truth in his eyes and then she pulled his face to her chest, finger-combing his hair.

"May I ask why?" she said.

"It's a big world," he whispered. "I can't be staying around here forever."

"Please," she said, but before she could say more they were startled by a knock at the kitchen door.

"It's me," came a muffled voice, and then another knock.

It was Mercy at the kitchen door, the vapor of her breath, the silver-brook of moonlight making her skin so pale.

"Don't answer," he said, but already his mother was turning on the outside light and unlocking the door.

"Look who's here," she said, ushering Mercy into the kitchen.

"What are you doing here?" he said, looking at her with surprise and distrust. Her hair was short and raggedly cut. Her eyes were red and swollen from crying and no matter how hard he tried he could not temper the severity of his reaction.

"I was wondering how long you were going to avoid me," Mercy said, her voice barely a whisper.

"I am sorry," Clemmie said to Mercy. "I don't feel very well. Perhaps you'll visit again?" She clutched at her robe and went up the stairs.

"Are you angry at me?" Mercy said.

"You should go," he said.

"I have something for you," she said, holding out her clasped hand. "What will you do with it when you have it?"

"How can I say if I don't know what it is?"

"Give me your hand," she said, and when he gave her his hand, she said, "It's a good hand, Henry Childs," and then she gave it back to him with a folded piece of paper.

He unfolded the piece of paper to see the drawing of a heart shot with an arrow. The initials were his and hers.

"What's this?"

"A gift."

"To me?"

"To you."

She then spoke of her love for him as if it was a distant country full of wonders and she had recently arrived. She did not know what happened to him today, but she knew what happened to herself.

"I'm sorry," he said, but inside him was something hard, pitiless and cold.

"What is it?" she said. "Say it."

But he made no reply. His hands felt thick and heavy and he could not move them.

"Answer me," she said. "Say something."

"I am sorry," he said again.

Her face softened. "When I first met you, I thought you were nice. But you aren't. It's just your face and it's inside you you're cold."

Henry said nothing.

"Nothing makes a dent in you," she said.

"Your heart is not so soft," he said. "It was you in that automobile watched it happen."

"I don't know what you are talking about."

"You are a liar," Henry said. "Can't you see, I don't love you anymore."

"Yes," she said. "Yes, you do."

"No, I don't."

"God damn you," she said. "I have told you I love you. What more can I say?"

There was the sound of someone at the top of the stairs, his mother. Mercy placed her hands on his hips and he watched her mouth open as she could not catch her breath. When the sound upstairs went silent she raised her face to his and she kissed him and he kissed her back.

"I am going," she whispered into his ear. "The car is packed and I am going whether you want to come or not."

He would remember feeling his way along the unlighted back hall and in his room packing a satchel of clothes. His bag in hand, he paused at his mother's door, his heart like the wing beating of a bird, but did not knock.

"You are going?" he heard her say from behind her door. There was no worry in his mother's voice and he could not understand that. He opened her door and stepped inside as she lit the lamp on the nightstand and propped herself with a pillow. In the shaded white light there was a pain ghosting her face.

At her window he touched the glass with his fingertips. He let his palm go flat on its cold surface. Outside was the moon inside a pale circle amid the eddying stars. She reached over and switched off the light and then he told her he was running away with Mercy and he did not want her to be worried about him.

"Take her, then," his mother said. "Before it's too late. You never want to find out it is too late in life."

"I think it's what I want," he said.

"Is it so complicated?"

"She said she wasn't there today. She wasn't inside her father's automobile."

"She wasn't," his mother said, and he turned from the window to face her. She'd pressed her wrist to her mouth.

He could see how sorry and tired her eyes, could hear it in her breath.

"It was me," she said. "I was in the backseat. I was the one."

He put his face in his hands. The shudders came and went and he was left empty and tired.

"I did not want you hurt," she said. Her face silvered in the darkness and her eyes burned into him.

He scarcely dared breathe. The longer he stood there, the less he knew what to say, and then he lied and told her he knew she was the one and he knew it was because she did not want him to get hurt.

"I love you," he said, and he kissed her right hand and then her left and then she spoke in a bare whisper.

"I love you too," she said and his heart was as if a thin cry.

In the desperation of his mind he'd not thought of his mother and he'd not thought of Mercy and felt himself alone and to be surrounded by misery. But now he knew.

"You asked after my dream," she said, her face pale and red eyed. "I am afraid this was my night's dream and now I cannot escape it."

She left her bed and from the bottom drawer of her bureau unwrapped a cloth bundle that held a knife with a white jigged bone handle and then she unwrapped another cloth to reveal a pistol. She wrapped them again and placed them in his hands. She told him they'd belonged to his old uncle and now they were his and he was to take them with him where he was going.

Chapter 7

THE MORNING HAD BEEN uneventful, even pleasant at times. Mercy was hatless and looked very beautiful with the sun on her face.

He would remember it was a day in June and the red iron sun made the heat dazzle in the air. The wind through the open windows was only so cooling as to measure the sweat on their skin, and the weather being clement, they put the top down and the light became fantastic.

He was driving the Mercury and trying to get as much distance between where they were and where they no longer wanted to be. Mercy was riding beside him and yet for them it was two different places they occupied and he imagined it would always be so.

Now that Mercy's hair was cut short she would no doubt be mistook by some to be a young boy. She wore blue jeans, a black and red flannel shirt and work boots scuffed blond as pine and stained from the muck and manure of the stables. Her clothes and boots smelled of the horse barn, but it wasn't a few hours down the road before she became the very spirit of flight. She raised her chin until the angle of the sun's rays were perpendicular to her face.

She moaned and at first he was not sure why, but then he understood it was simple and overwhelming pleasure.

"Let's make our own life," she said. "Let's not go back until we're old."

She lay across the seat with her head in his lap and slept in those early hours of flight, making small movements and small sounds. In sleep her fists would clench and then open and then they would clench again. He held her to him and the sounds would subside and then after a while they would start up again and he could feel the rage that was inside him.

"Would your father ever let that happen?" he asked.

She did not say anything but responded with a look of fear and anxiety and he thought he'd never hated so virulently. He tried to understand but couldn't. He'd never wanted to fight someone and beat them down as he did now.

"It is a conversation I do not want to have," she said, and then after a time, she said, "I miss the Gaylen horse most of all."

As the land flattened and dulled, constant was the mirage of water, blurring and gaseous, and in his head came a clicking sound for some miles and he thought it to be a feature of flatness, or an attribute of mirage, or caused by the blanketing heat until finally he found a throbbing vein in his forehead and pressed his finger to the skin lest it burst and fill his eyes.

Henry let his hand rest on Mercy's shoulder. Then he reached down and not wanting to wake her, he slowly pulled up her shirt. He wanted the skin of her back. He had studied her back and learned the names of its parts, and while she slept, and beneath the rucked cloth, he trailed his fingers along the vertebrae that supported her skull, that held her head erect when she stood. He counted her ribs, those long slender spines on heart-shaped bodies and the lumbar of her column, curved, erect, mobile, balanced. Sometimes he thought the only reason to love her was her back.

Henry pulled over and held Mercy to him as the engine idled and she came out of her dream. Long ago they'd come down from the mountains and crossed the moatlike Ohio River, its surface shiny and combustible. She flexed her body into his, her face to his belly as if inside was something precious she'd lost and then found. She bore no marks from her past, but inside she was like knotted ropes. He held her as tightly as he dared, which was as tightly as he could and felt for the deep muscles of her back, his left hand to the latissimus wrapping under her ribs and his right hand passing over top her deltoid to the teres major. She sighed and went back for better dreams, or no dreams at all, and he thought how holding her was holding himself.

In her sleep she fetched his hand inside her shirt front to cover her breast and then with her own hand she covered his lap and told him to please keep driving. She wanted him not to be tired but to drive the car and take them away. They were bound for New Orleans where the Mississippi was yellow in the sunlight and slow running behind its high levees. They would live their days in New Orleans, shy and hidden away.

They crossed the Ohio again and at a diner they ordered milkshakes, strawberry and vanilla, and hamburgers and fries. When they were asked to change tables for no apparent reason they looked at each other, suspicious of the simplest request. Henry scanned the diner for a face he might recognize, a man or woman, a couple eyeing them, and then turning to confer, maybe it'd be her brother or father. But he did not fix on anyone so his mind gave up the thought and did not care who it was or who it could be or what they wanted.

I'm not nobody, he thought, and reached across the table so she might twine her fingers with his.

That night they took a room on the Natchez Trace, all those thick vines and Spanish moss hung by live oak and catalpa outside the room, running alongside the walls. When she went to turn off the radio, he told her to leave it on because he liked to sleep with sound in the room.

"You are like a little baby that way," she said. "The way little babies like to have sound when they sleep."

"Then turn it off," Henry said.

"No," she said. "I was only teasing."

Soon after they fell asleep, he awoke to Mercy making sound again and her body articulating that sound. It was like a cry or a whimper and then she woke with a fright, and when she turned on the light they discovered it was her time of month and she'd bled onto the sheets. She insisted they strip the bed and rinse out the sheets and hang them from the shower rod and they spent the rest of that night on the mattress covered with a blanket.

In the morning he awoke to find her sleeping atop him. She woke too and asked him if it was morning.

"What we are doing is not right. We should go back," Mercy said. "I need to sort things out."

In that moment he could no longer imagine another future.

"Don't do that," she said. "Don't be that way. My determination is fixed to have you."

She took his face in her hands. She was telling him her words were true and she was desperate he understand.

Henry thought how all life must be strange and fantastic to Mercy, life without limitations. Hers was the charmed life.

Then he was alone and she was gone to make a phone call. Is this love, he wondered, and why did it make him feel so alone even when he was with her? He did not know if he understood what she wanted from him.

"What are you thinking?" she said when she returned. He was dressed and his satchel was packed and he was smoking a cigarette in a chair by the door.

"Nothing. I was just away in my mind."

"Can't remember?"

"No. Not really," he said, and it was true, he could not remember.

"My father," she said, going down on her knees. "He is a thoroughly bad man."

In his mind he repeated her words and thought for the first time his own father might be the same, a bad man. It was then he understood his hatred of Mercy's father, the distillate of so long a love, a hatred, a never knowing who his father was. He'd not so much cared before now, but now he did.

"You can leave me here," he said. "I will keep going on my own."

"I am always saying the wrong thing," she said, and raised her hand from his knee to her mouth as if next time to catch the words. He felt her leaning toward him as she spoke. Her words came restive and urgent, as if more for herself, and they incited a dull aching restlessness inside him.

"I am ready," she said, reaching around his waist. "We can go now."

"Did you make your phone call?"

"I have given you my heart," she said. "I am your own forever."

"Is that so?" Henry said.

"I promise."

"Who did you call?"

"I called Walter to tell him we wouldn't be there."

Nothing more was said and they did not talk about it again. He was thinking of love as if it were a place and not a person, not an emotion of the human kind, but where you stood and in the air you breathed. His mind was hopeless with the mystery of her, struggling for reasons why she did what she did.

Outside their room the sunlit mist was a cloud of light. Before them was the long stretch of southwest highway, the roadsides rampant with vine and so hot the asphalt quaked and fumed.

Chapter 8

DEEPER INTO THE SOUTH they descended, riding over
the dissolving ammoniac land, its smells of sawdust and
urine, past deserted shacks and abandoned stations, churches
fallen in on themselves, sawmills, outhouses, bayous, piney
woods. In the trembling heat, he felt their longing and rapture,
their ruin, their persuading death. All day he was haunted by
the morning's sudden turn and return. All day was humid
and the throb and stink of decay gathered as if from the entire
earth. The lush and flaring grass of the planted levees, the ra-
diating, suspiring earth rising and sinking.

At a little store they stopped for gasoline and a pack of
cigarettes, the hand pumps shaded by cottonwoods, the fluff
of their catkins filling the air. Beyond the highway, past the
brake fern was mud and muck and wetness. Little boys were
swimming in the still water flats and when they stood they
were naked in the unclear light of the brilliant sun. They held
aloft the fish they'd caught, fat and alive.

Inside the little store, its floor skiffed with sawdust, the old
woman at the cash box was black, her skin almost purple, her
eyes milky white and shaded blue as a robin's egg. Behind
her were broken cartons of Camels, Chesterfields, Kools,

and open packs she sold by the cigarette. There were dusty bottles of Four Roses whisky and gallon jars of pickled eggs and ham hocks and sausages. A crutch hung by the door. In the shadowed back was a propped-up billiard table with three mahogany legs and leather pockets. Other blacks, men in their shirtsleeves, sat under the waves of a slowly nicking ceiling fan. They looked to be eating from a platter of chicken livers and drinking out of jelly glasses they filled from a stoppered jug.

A girl wearing a pink cotton blouse came in with a bucket of ice.

"Come here, girl," one of the men said, and when she was near he handed her a silver dollar.

A man with a cardboard suitcase bound with baling twine stepped up and asked him which way he was heading. He was long boned and as if built of pipe. On both cheeks he wore perfect scars that ran to the corners of his mouth. Henry told the man he was headed south and the man smiled and his scars rose and slowly he shook his head.

"No. No. No," he said as he conducted the air with a shaking hand. "That is the wrong answer," he said, and the other men laughed and guffawed.

As they came out of the store they were offered and declined the fish the boys had caught, moist in a bucket under a gunnysack. Mercy handed them a few dollars anyway and told them they could sell their fish to someone else.

The evening was a cloudless sky and the setting sun cast a bluish twilight on the land as they traveled an endless cut through piney woods beside railroad tracks. Overhead was a hot starry night and the white strip of highway seemed to glow in the bending light.

To the west the clouds were gray over gray and a mizzle-rain began to fall in the shineless black. Henry pulled over for a spell. He felt alone and he felt the loneliness of responsibility. Mercy stirred in the seat beside him.

"Hush now," he said. "You sleep while I rest a minute."

He let his head back and closed his eyes. The sound of an automobile at high speed woke him, the driver blaring his horn. The darkness was thinning with the climbing moon, the windshield wet with rain and fogged with the rising mist. The cottonwoods seemed waiting and unwhispering in the hot air. To look back was to lessen a sense of belonging where he was. He thought of the knife and pistol in the bottom of his satchel. When he awoke again she was looking at him. She stuck out her tongue and crossed her eyes.

The mist had filled the pockets and there was a great winding sound, a bore of sound, and when the train came it came right at them and she screamed before it bent off. It was as if the bluish fog clung to the roaring clatter and hiss of steam the engines poured. They drove on until they saw lights and bumped across the tracks and stopped at a motor court, its neon sign flickering in the darkness.

"This morning about broke me," he said as he kicked off his boots. The miles he'd driven still thrummed in his hands and arms and his thoughts could no longer be restrained.

"Don't talk about bad things. Talk about good things."

"You don't want me," he said. "I don't have anything."

"I have been waiting for someone to come along and it

may as well be you," she whispered. Her voice was warm and honeyed.

"Don't be funny," Henry said.

"I would be so lonely without you," she said.

"No," he said.

"Don't get sore," Mercy said.

"We never really got to know each other," he said.

"We know each other."

"What about you? Where are you getting to?"

"I don't think about it like that. No, I don't."

"What did Walter say?" he said after a while.

"He said he'd manage and we were to have fun."

She slipped her feet from her sandals and put them in his lap where he held her dusty ankles and dirty feet.

"Take your clothes off," she said, and when he did she slid her hand inside his thigh.

"I want my baby back in my arms," she said.

"You're already aswim with me," he said.

"I know," she said. "I can feel it," and she moved as if the feeling went through her body. Her body contracted and released and she squeezed his thigh and he could feel her nails.

"You want it now?" he said.

"Anytime," she said. "Always."

He hovered over her, her eyes a distant gaze, empty and blissful. She told him the day had been a very long time and then she licked her tongue over his nipple. The bed began to shake and there was a roar, another long northbound freight rasping the tracks, the train shuddering to a stop. Then he spent himself and felt within the collapse of his spending.

"That's a bull's-eye," she said.

In the morning they stepped again into the tangled land, and wet and radiant, the morning's purple horizon. They were parked beside an abandoned depot where the earth was strewn with oil drums and tipped-over milk cans, broken crockery, rusted-out washtubs, a snake. He suddenly flashed on a vision of disaster: women weeping and children and men dying, and it filled him.

"Henry," she said. She was shaking him by the arm, her silver bracelets jangling. "Henry, what's come over you?" she said. This day she wore a starched white dress and twine sandals and smelled of talcum.

"Nothing," he said. "I am okay."

"You look like you seen a ghost."

"Let's get out of here."

He unlocked Mercy's door and opened it for her. He unlocked his own and set the pistol in its cloth bundle on the floor behind his seat.

The clammy mist turned crimson. Mercy propped her feet on the dashboard and wiggled her newly painted toenails. The air was heating and the day was like the two halves of what you are and they were split open like a chest with no attending surgeon to hover the interior.

Chapter 9

THERE WAS WHERE THEY'D been and there was where they were going and Henry was haunted by the feeling this was the last of all roads on earth and if not for the two of them, then surely it would be the last for him.

"I like being this close to you," Mercy said, clasping his arm as he drove the long highway parallel to the great river.

He was tired and wanted to sleep. He wanted to harbor. He thought how he wanted to finish his days on an island some distance off any coast on any ocean and to die by the roar of the sea and let it wash his body with its sand bearing water over and over.

"I belong to you," she said, impatient and wanting him to talk. "There just isn't any two ways around it. You are mine and I am yours."

"I am a fool," he said.

"I love fools," she said, swinging her legs across his lap and her arm at his neck, "because they believe that anything can happen. I am about sure I was made for you."

She wondered aloud on what it would be like where they were going. They'd take their meals on an iron balcony and eat above the airless streets below. There would be the smell of flowers under the balcony. Everyday would be a parade of sorts: beads and balloons, straw hats, plastic windmills, bubble pipes.

"How about saying a road prayer," she asked, yawning and stretching. He nodded and so she prayed into his ear that they would have very good weather and have a safe journey and arrive soon and then she said her amen and then she said, "Please, God, watch over us."

She let herself back to sleep on the seat, her legs in his lap and though he wanted sleep too and was dreadfully tired, he could not sleep because he was driving and did not want to stop. He was going to a place where he had never been before and for him it was like the cord of fate.

Hours later, it was nighttime again and the moon was rising just over the trees and darkness was coming on when the Mercury started to overheat. Mercy came awake, wiping the sleep from her eyes as the automobile coughed and slowed. A strap on her dress had fallen from her shoulder uncovering her breast. She held her hands to her chest and had begun to shiver. He pulled her close to his side.

"Why are you shaking?" he asked her. "Are you cold?"

"It is the presence of God," Mercy said. "He was here."

"I don't think God has ever been to this place."

"God is ever'where," she said.

"My mother told me it was God created us because he was lonely. They say he was like a beautiful jewel and he wanted to be appreciated and so he created us."

"That is a very pretty thought."

"I do not think she meant it to be."

She looked at him as if he were a mental, so he agreed to consider more seriously the existence of God and suggested that God could perhaps make a modest first step by curing what ailed the Mercury.

"He doesn't mind you," she said. "You go ahead and play all you want and he'll just play right along."

The Mercury juddered and lurched and with each lurch his blood quickened. Henry thought if worse came to worst, they could walk away from this automobile. They could un-screw the license plates and throw them in the swamp. They could take Mercy's suitcase from the trunk, and his satchel, and hitchhike out of there to anywhere but where they were and disappear into the darkness. But they continued through the night, the automobile overheated more and more.

"We are soon to be broke down," Henry warned Mercy, slow as child talk.

"I want to get a room," she said, "and go to sleep in a nice soft bed. Then I want to get up and have a bath and a nice breakfast."

"We are a long way from anywhere," he said.

"Who cares?" she said to the windshield. She turned to look out her side into the blackness that was no longer rush-ing by but was slowed to pulse and night heat as they lurched along.

"I want you to tear my clothes off," she said.

"You're just trying to cheer me up," he said.

"You know what I want," she said. She was getting sulky and was determined to have her way. They were bound by the need that comes when you are the only two left and you

are bound by decisions you cannot change, cannot even remember making.

"I want you to keep doing what you started," Mercy said.

He held to the wheel with both hands. He thought, how
to say the words, how to tell her the confusion in his mind.

"I do not want to make love or whatever word you call
down."

"What do you want?"

"I want everything."

"For that, I'll promise you anything," she whispered. "But
you will have to do it now."

Henry jammed his foot onto the accelerator and they pulled
off the highway across a creek and limped into an open field,
the transmission screaming with melting heat. They stopped
in the darkness where deer picked up their heads and flared
away to the forest. He lifted up her dress on the front seat and
it was as if big stars were bursting inside his head. They fixed
to each other in the darkness and he wished that tonight was
all the healing and the blessing a body needed and had been
promised these thousands of years.

They unfurled a blanket in the grass under the smoky
moonlight, under the black sky and the ink black clouds,
and he got a hunger for food and a thirst for water but also a
feeling of never wanting food or water again. Their skin went
cool in the wet air and their bodies were slick with sweat.

She took his hand and held it to her body, moving it from
place to place, and he felt the rise and seep of her body's sweet
waters, the fast blood inside his own body and for a moment
they were as close as the hand to the water it passes through.

"Will you make love to me again," Mercy said, scratching her nails at his back.

"That's not what this is anymore," he said, but she was still coming on, still driven by whatever she could possibly do that would make her a part of him. She propped her bare heels on the high round of the tire and cocked her pelvis in the air. She dragged his thigh under her wet ass to hold her up.

"I think you struck bottom," she said in her plaintive voice, and she placed his hand in the wetness between her legs like it was a little bird fallen from its nest.

"I hope so," he said, and he had the idea he was taking them into hell. He was the rock and he was rushing to the bottom and she was tethered to him and he was drowning them down deep in the water.

"Henry," she whispered, and he pulled her tighter and tucked her in alongside him, sad for how much he needed her and did not trust her. He felt like a child in bed come from nightmare. He was alone with her with this broken-down automobile on the earth of a southern field and she had come from her father's house and it seemed so long ago when they first set out.

"I do love God," Mercy said, "the way he made everything."

"Please hush," he said. "Not now. We have to get up and get in the automobile. I'll find us some water for the radiator."

In the trunk he found a gallon can and went down the road bank to fill it with the brackish water of a stagnant slough. When he returned, he unlatched the hood and slung it open. In the darkness, he located the radiator cap and twisted it. Instantly, from the depths of its coils, there came a great burst of steam and boiling water that spewed flat and then blew forth.

I have just been stupid, he thought as the radiator's hot geyser burned his arms and galled his naked chest and then caught the side of his face.

Chapter 10

ONE EYE CLOSED AND would not open as he stepped back and tumbled in the bracken. He screamed from the scalding water on his skin like something raw and unformed and mortally wounded. He got himself up and ran to the water's edge and threw himself in.

There was a great splash and flounce of water when his body hit and his mind blacked and then went red, and then slowly the world came to him and he was surfacing and spitting slimy water from out his mouth and nose. She was down on her knees, waist deep in the water, and she was holding him up.

"Let me go," he croaked, and every time she did, he put himself under again and felt for rocks and weeds to hold so she had to fight him to pull him back to the air he hated.

"Are you okay," she kept saying, and he could tell she was unhappy with herself for saying such, but she could find nothing else to say to him. "Henry," she cried, "let me help you."

Finally the burning dulled and was no more than another worst pain he'd ever experienced. He crawled on his knees, panting with one fixed eye. He hobbled, dazed and clumsy, and she kept a shoulder under his arm, saying they needed to get to a hospital, but he told her no to that as he lurched and staggered.

They filled and capped the radiator and the engine started. She had to drive because he couldn't see well enough. They entered the highway again and after a few miles came to a little gas station and grocery store. Mercy banged on the door until a light went on and an old man shuffled from a backroom, dragging his suspenders onto his shoulders. She bought gas and oil and a sealing mixture to pour in the radiator. She bought a salve that promised to relieve the pain of scalding burns.

Shirtless, Henry lay back in the passenger's seat and she spread the salve on his face and chest. However hard she tried to hide her concern, he could tell by her face that he was badly burned, but for the moment he was soothed.

This time he slowly uncapped the radiator under a clutch of rags. It was not so fierce as before, but its heat was terrifying. He poured in the sealing mixture and more water. He replaced the cap and slammed shut the hood.

"You need to see a doctor," she said. "It is what you are supposed to do."

"We can go now," he said. She hesitated until he said, "Now, God damn it," and so she drove while he navigated.

Hours later, they chugged into the outskirts of New Orleans and the headlights raised up shacks and shotgun houses. The houses were small and well tended and inside each was a darkness more black than the night itself. The automobile was breaking down again, becoming noisy and recalcitrant and soon would be of no use to them.

"Henry," she said. "I know where I am. We're almost there, baby."

It was then he began to cry silently. It filled his throat and caught there. Inside him there came thousands of breakings and tightenings. Inside him, a noose cinched taut and he felt for breath.

When he awoke they were parked and she was in the back-seat sleeping beside him. He put his arm around her and she curled and folded inside his hands.

"Are you ready for again?" she said, her stirring at his side making his burns go hot.

He made a laughing sound and gathered her ardent turn-ing body in his arms, the touch of her burning him, and hove up on his knees as if to pray, as if he were the last man in the land and she were this woman under him, the last female of his kind and half of him was on fire again. He wanted to be so good when he felt so black inside.

She lifted her dress up over her hips.

The soon-to-be light was still off in the east and inside his hands he held her ribs, the swoop of her white spine. She reached back between her legs to where they fit and sighed and said his name again and again.

Their skin was greasy, his stung and boiled, and he was pulsing and breathing and his heart pumping blood. Turning inside him was something like greatness. It shivered down his arms and the whole of him was on fire. He set off inside her and he thought maybe that was the one and maybe with that they would be together forever.

She returned herself to his side and closed her eyes and

passed into something like sleep, but he was left raw and burned and awake. He thought how much he must be hated by her father and he hated him back. He had come along with her, both of them leaving their families behind. He did not know how bound she was to hers or even if she was bound to them at all. Sometimes he thought she'd found him so that he would take her away. That was fine with him.

She whispered, "You opened my body and took out all my bones starting with the small ones."

She lay against him, the scant light rising on her neck, her body rigid.

"Did it happen yet?" he asked, and was no more than a gasping whisper as his hand floated before his good eye and settled between her legs.

"Oh, yes. I have a feeling," she said. "I believe that was the one that made a new little baby."

"Do you think a boy or a girl?" he asked.

"I don't know. It has not decided yet. You know they take a little while to decide and even then they can change their minds."

The light was coming on and there were new shadow lines and he could make out streets canopied in trees.

"This is the place?" he said, and he thought how greasy their skin in the warm sultry air, the darkness like velvet. He thought how far from home, from the stables, from the mountain, from the Gaylen horse.

"Not yet," she said, and told him they needed to wait a little bit longer and pick up a key.

Chapter 11

I N NEW ORLEANS THERE was a second-floor apartment owned by an old woman, a relation of Mercy's with whom she'd conspired to make her escape. They entered a courtyard and went down a cindered path. They entered again and waited in a high-ceilinged foyer until the door cracked open. The caretaker, a gray-haired woman, had glasses that magnified her eyes. When Mercy explained who they were, she smiled and let them in. She told them she was expecting them.

Inside the paint was peeling and the plaster spalling. The floor was stained with watermarks and the carpets were mildewed and pitted with cigarette burns. When she returned with the keys, she told Mercy she'd cleaned and stocked the pantry and the icebox. The linens were fresh and if she needed anything, anything at all, just to come by and she would see to it. She handed Mercy an envelope that was addressed to her. Inside there was an affectionate letter from her aunt with a number of hundred-dollar bills in the fold.

The door to their apartment was painted red. Henry fitted the key in the lock and turned and pushed it open. The apartment they entered was painted gold with white wainscoting, the curtains violet, the scrims transparent. Upholstered in pale matching silks were two sofas, two armchairs, and four side chairs and a center table.

Their rooms had tall palladium windows, storm shutters, and a balcony with a railing and there were flowerpots in the corners. In their upstairs rooms, the floor was covered with sweetgrass and there were sachets of honeysuckle in every drawer. The bedroom was a painted mural, bowers of full-blown roses. There was a canopy bed, a bureau, and a high-boy. There were votive candles in the cupboards to light, to keep them dry of mildew. All about the rooms were Chinese porcelains encircled with dragons, marble statues slim in head, throat, and feet. There were mirrors framed in flames or shell-like curves, or wrapped in reeds and palms, a wall clock entwined in leafy melting branches. Where the sweet-grass separated, the floor was sticky to their feet and the soles of their shoes peeled with each step. The rooms were the spirit of a merely beautiful world: gilded, disfigured, and enchanted. They were softness and prettiness, the scene of their new existence. It smelled like brown sugar and they had a view of churches through the spreading.

Over the days she applied a salve and Henry's burns healed. In the closets were lace and antique clothes, satin high heels, bias-cut slinks, a black and ivory satin halter gown, chiffon bedroom coats and jackets. Mercy tried them on one by one and sashayed about the rooms, her head held high. The clothes caressed the curves of her body and rippled when she walked and it was as if she were clothed in water.

These fashion shows were the prelude to making love and

at this they were very good. They would go until their hips were bruised and their bodies were thinned and dry and tasted salty. The room dark and hot and Mercy in a white slip and wearing lipstick, the sun setting down the east wall. He watched her as she sat on the tub wall and lifted her skirt to unclasp her stockings and slide them down her legs. Then she stood and, with her skirt still raised, slid her garter belt over her hips. At the sink she washed out her stockings and hung them over the shower curtain.

"What did you do today?" she said.

"I wandered about some."

"What did you see?"

"I watched a dog eat a bee," he said.

With a pick he chipped ice and filled tall glasses with the shards. Mercy draped her arms over his shoulders. The scrims lifted in a brief wind and then settled as he quartered and divided again a lemon.

"Let's move on," Henry whispered.

"Where is better than here?" she asked, taking a step back.

"Maybe Texas. Maybe California."

"But that's so far from home," she said.

"But isn't that what we're doing? Running away?"

"This love will take care of us."

When words were no longer enough, they took up where they left off with their lovemaking and they stayed in New Orleans because for her it seemed far enough from home. Those days in New Orleans were half bronze and half dream — to be in love and to be loved forever, and to be taken care of by that love.

In the still hours of the morning, Mercy looked up from his shoulder and a scream caught in her throat. She pointed and he turned to see a man standing outside the window. The man was pointing at them and he was smiling. He wore the headgear of a jester and a multicolored suit festooned with white flickering lights. He was not standing on their balcony or propped to a ladder but was walking in the street.

"Look," she said, her fright turning to laughter. "There's a clown outside the window."

She drew the sheet to cover her nakedness and Henry went to the opening in the wall where the lighted man stood. Outside was a man on stilts and there were dozens more and another man, smaller of stature, though who could know, and he was yelling at the stilt walkers through a megaphone trying to get them into some kind of order as if rehearsing for a parade. The stilt walker outside their window bowed contritely asking forgiveness. Henry nodded and the man smiled and stilt-walked his way into line.

That morning they came down from their rooms and entered into the Quarter. The air was thick and near to suffocating, so dense it was like a great stone inside his chest vying with his lungs for space. They entered a small chapel and there they were married and it became something they would do several more times for they found it to be a salutary experience.

When they returned, they sat on the balcony and ate oranges and grapefruit. Tank wagons came through with water hoses, washing the streets and raising up the sour smell of liquor and urine left from the night before, and crews of black men followed the trucks, sweeping water and trash and smell before them. Shortly after they passed by their balcony, the air was clean and the sun shone a little brighter.

"I think that's a job I could do," Henry said.

"Don't be silly," she said.

"Still," he said, "I should ask."

"If you were to ask to do such a job, not only would they turn you away, they would be suspicious."

"But I ought to have a job."

"I don't want you working," Mercy said, and explained that when he was away from her, her back would go to fire and her nerves would fray.

"Besides," she said, "of late, I have considered giving up the act of walking and if I decide to I would need you here to carry me from room to room."

"I'll work at night while you sleep," Henry said.

"Then who will watch over me? I want my husband to stay with me."

"What about money?" Henry said.

"We have plenty of money, enough for both of us for a long time."

"What happens when that runs out?"

"I have enough relatives who hate my father and they will give us what we need."

ON MONDAYS THEY ate red beans and rice and in the afternoons they ate beignets and drank café au lait. There was a black man with blue cataracts who drew their portraits in charcoal for a dime. By day, the Quarter was alternately suffused with calmness and torrid heat, and the day was like a wetted rag with the scent of sugars and syrups, coffee and animal. In the evenings pastel shadows moved across the old brick, and slices of shadow appeared behind the wrought-iron balconies, dapples of shadows on the cobbles in the street. Some nights there were soldiers in the street. They would get drunk and begin fighting and be hauled off to the riot pens. Mercy would light candles and they'd lie awake, listening to the guttering flames, aswim in the thick liquid air, the jazz music, the brawls in the streets.

One evening they were passing through an alley when they saw a drunk man, narrow shouldered and buck toothed being questioned by a cop. It was the same man who'd drawn their portraits and Henry started to say something, but Mercy stopped him. The cop struck at the man's hip pocket with a billy club to break the bottle he carried and whisky ran down the man's pant leg. Again, Henry was to say something, but Mercy took his arm and urged him away. In that moment he understood how afraid she was of any encounter that might reveal them, her secrecy, her insistence upon locking the door.

"The police. Stay away from them," she said, and he knew enough to not ask why.

Mercy began working on a book she was making and he would watch her gliding fingers as they scissored paper and taped and drew and painted. It was a large book with a hard black cover and sheets of thick paper and when she turned the pages they made great sweeping noises as if the paper still had memory of the wood it fell from. He listened to the scratch of her pencil and over her shoulder he could see drawings and paintings. There were faint letters, words, and numbers. She knew he was there and would let him look but not for so long before she would chase him away.

He asked about one page and she told him she was writing a poem for every part of her body. On another page she said the image was nothing in particular but came from her mind and made little sense, but soon she would figure it out. The signs were as if a foreign language had been encoded by a nonspeaker, twice and thrice removed from understanding, and there were scribblings and washes and recipes, figures, fashion, algebraic calculations, and reminders of things to do.

As the days passed Mercy began keeping more pages wholly unto herself and beyond his understanding. She would let Henry have glimpses and he would see a list of things to get at the market and be relieved but then another page without shape or form. She told him they were inside the book together and if she ever disappeared he would find her there, and then she shooed him away.

Chapter 12

ONE DAY HE WENT out and when he came back Mercy was weeping. She held a letter in one hand and an envelope in the other. It was a moment that bordered on the frightful because she had been eating pistachio nuts and her fingers and her mouth and about her mouth were red with stain and so too her eyes where she had wiped at them.

"Why would someone say these things to me?" she begged to know, her red fingers fluttering in the air as she spoke.

He looked at the envelope and there was no name and the letter itself was addressed to no one in particular. She told him she was working and happened to look down and saw where it had been slipped under the door.

He asked what it said and she read.

When I saw you, I knew I needed to tell you that I floated on that very same dinghy you're on in that same vast ocean. I'll tell you what I've learned firsthand about God. What he wants is to become more real to you than anything else in the world. His friendship will be like none you have ever known or will ever know again. He will talk to you just like a friend with skin would and your heart

will know it is him talking. You will be astounded at the
things he reveals about himself, others and about you. You
will know it is his voice if it is full of love and encourage-
ment, wisdom and humor. He does not speak King James
English. The other angry condemning voices you hear are
not his.

"Who wrote it?" Henry asked.

"The old woman with the glasses. I went to the balcony and saw her come out."

"She wants to save you."

"But I am not lost."

"No," Henry said. "You are with me."

"Do you think she's crazy?"

"What are you getting at?"

"Do you think she'll do something?"

"No."

"What about this?" Mercy said, waving the sheet of paper.

Henry suggested she put the letter in one of her books and she seemed to brighten at the idea. She asked him to help her and he did, brushing glue onto a blank page, while she trimmed the edges of the letter and then damping its back with glue, together they pressed it down into the book, her hands overtop his. Then he held her and rocked her in his arms.

"We are set in stone," she said. "We are bound and forever will be."

That night they walked down by the river past the tall black iron fences, the black iron columnades and from off the river was the gentle invitation of evening wind.

That morning Henry saw a woman jump into the river and disappear. She put her purse down near the levee and walked out on the rocks and jumped in. She then swam toward the middle of the river and disappeared in the fog. Birds were skimming the mystic dazzling surface and Henry watched her as she disappeared into the milky light. There was a man by the river and he observed to him what had just happened.

"Oh," the man had said, "she seems to be a real good swimmer."

"Where is she swimming to?" he'd asked.

"One time she made it to the other side, but the current took her several blocks downstream."

"But she has disappeared," Henry said.

"Maybe you should tell someone, but I've seen her do it before. She's a real good swimmer. I can't say, but it seemed like her own idea and you've got to 'spect that."

As they approached the place there was a gathering of people where the woman had entered the water and farther out a trolling boat.

"She's drowned," Mercy said.

"I am afraid of that," he said.

"We can't do anything about it," she said. "We should but we can't." Her words were her thoughts tumbling from her mind.

Henry took her in his arms, but she pulled free and stood alone. He took her again and held her tightly and when she softened and breathed into his chest he guided her away from the river.

Their days remained as such, released into the hush of

indeterminate time, the world poised at the strange edge. There was no clock, no calendar that moored them in the stream of nights that begot days and days that drifted into darkness. It was as if they'd broken time itself and there was only waiting. Waiting for light and darkness, waiting for sunrise and sunset.

Then came the day he convinced her to let him work and send money to Clemmie, because he'd always contributed a share to their existence. Mercy had of late been restless and changeable, plunging into long meditative silences and then for no perceptible reason engaging him again.

"I understand," she said. "If you must."

So he took work cleaning an office building just completed and being readied for the occupants. His partner was a Haitian named Paul, a black-skinned man, not tall, but ebullient and, as he did not speak English, made for good company.

When Henry came back after work that first day, Mercy was in bed, crying. She told him that she was having bad thoughts and had decided against any future absence on his part.

"I'm afraid," she said.

"Of what?" he asked, taking her feet in his hands and holding them to his chest.

"That one day you won't come back." She curled her toes to clutch at his fingers and then released her hold.

"But you know I will," he said.

"I am afraid they will steal me while you are gone. Don't you see? He will steal me and lock me up."

"No," he said, moving to take her in his arms. "Nobody steals anybody. I will protect you."

"It's what he did to my mother."

He held her tightly in his arms and she let herself be comforted. He told her how much he loved her back and she told him how very much her back was in love with him.

"I have never been loved by a woman's back," he said.

"My back has changed since we have been together," she told him into his chest, and after a time they fell to sleep.

As each of the next few days went by she seemed less and less afraid at his morning departures. At work, he could not convince Paul it was okay to break at midmorning and take another break at noon for lunch, so he'd go down the stairs alone to the park across the street and wouldn't even be hungry but would sit in the sunlight and watch Paul in the empty windows across the street.

Paul's whole body would be framed in the big windows as he wetted the glass and stretched out his arms with rags in both hands and washed the windows and it would be as if he were washing the air itself as his hands swam before him. Henry would think of Mercy and wonder what he'd find when he climbed the stairs. She could rock back and forth for hours staring off to nowhere for long periods of time. He wondered sometimes if she'd even be there, or maybe she would be stolen away as she feared. And he missed Clemmie and felt a growing shame for leaving her.

One day at lunchtime, as Henry was occupying his bench, he could see where Paul had moved up a floor. Paul waved down to him and he waved back. Paul wetted the window with cleaning solution, and as if blessing the sky he began his white-handed circling, and then in the easiest way imaginable the window was coming out of the wall and he was coming with it. Four stories down, a tree fractured the diving sheet of glass and his fall broke through the branches and he lay there on the sidewalk like an upturned turtle, feebly waving his arms in the air as more glass rained down on him. His body was broken and blood was oozing from his mouth and the concrete around him sparkled with shards of shattered glass and shreds of green leaves.

For some reason Henry did not cross the street and he did not wait around. It wasn't such a hard thing to tell when someone is dead or about to be dead. He hurried away and back to the Quarter and climbed the stairs. The stairwell was dark and the lights would not work. He groped blindly through the upper hall and found their door. He dug up the key, let himself in, and locked the door behind him before he struck a match to find a candle.

Henry called out to Mercy, but she did not answer. She was gone and in her place he felt there to be another presence in the dark room, and at first he could not tell who it was and then he could. It was Randall standing in the shadows. He looked at Henry and then hit him over the head with a flat iron. Henry's vision exploded and blackened and he realized he may have gotten himself killed.

"It is over and you are not forgiven. Not now. Not ever."

The man's words seemed to be crossing a great distance on their way to Henry and were thick and slow.

"Jesus God, just don't hit me again," he cried. He could feel the cool wet of his own blood beginning to soak his hair.

"I don't want any of your back sass," Randall said, and he hit Henry again. Henry's vision blackened and then a noose dropped over his neck and a hand cinched it tight at his throat and from behind he was dragged onto his knees.

"It pays to be afraid," another voice said. The man's breath was hot and sour with tobacco. A stick match flared to light a cigar and then dropped to the floor where it slowly burned out.

"Go away," the voice said. "Don't ever come back."

Then he was alone. He lay on the floor, paralyzed in the shadowed light. His head was burning up with a pain it could not fully embrace and so it vined into his neck and shoulders and down into his chest. So great was the pain, he could not move to the bed. He touched at his head to feel wetness and came away with a slick of blood in his palm and leaking down his wrist.

Inside was a deep song he could not quite hear. Then there was the swashing of the blood in his heart and the hiss of air in his lungs and he knew that he was not dead. He held to the frayed end of the rope draped over his shoulder until he realized he was choking himself. He began to gasp and struggled to loosen the rope and let it drop to the floor.

She was gone and every trace of her. Gone was her black book. He could not peel back the fat rubber bands to open it, to reveal the pages for their codes and drawings, their faint letters, scribblings, and strange words. He could not go inside its pages to find her.

Left to him was the knife and the pistol, his inheritance

passed onto him by his mother's hand. She'd told him they were his and he was to take them with him where he was going.

It was as if a door had opened on hellfire and he had entered. He had the recurring sensation that a belt was ever tightening and loosening about his chest. He could not escape the feeling of entombment and no wish, no words, could change what had happened.

Part II

There on the perilous open
ground of war, in brave
expectancy they lay all night
while many campfires burned. As
when in heaven principle
stars shine out around the moon.

Iliad 8.626–31

Chapter 13

IT WAS OCTOBER 26, 1950, and harbored off the coast of North Korea were seventy-one transports packed with twenty-eight thousand marines waiting for the word to go.

In the early morning when the tide was right, they would climb down the nets into the landing craft, the flat-sided steel boats bucketing in the gray chop. A dirty rain had begun to fall on their shoulders. The air was rank with the smells of salt, paint, grease, tobacco, and sweat. Sky-bound soot and ash and brick dust were being dragged back to the earth and water from hazy suspension.

Some men took chaws out of their mouths and placed them in their caps while others retrieved the chaw they'd been saving and tucked it inside their cheek. Other men were sick and puked on their boots. Men squared their gear again. Men looked inside themselves for reason or meaning, but there was little there to be found. In their minds they dismantled and assembled their weapons again and again. They mouthed the words to prayers, and rosaries came out, the ticking beads entwining fingers grimed with Cosmoline. They cradled the little Jesus in the palm of a hand, whispered cadences, and for a moment Henry envied them their belief and passion. He envied them their pastoral moment for how unplaceable he felt himself to be. He was just seventeen.

Marine Corsairs heaved into view. They came as if phantoms from beyond the orbit of the moon, their inexorable motion of speed, their trailings of sublunar vapors, resizing every second, and suddenly there were vast and terrifying and devouring sound explosions tearing the sky and they disappeared.

Lew Devine took out his spearmint chewing gum, rolled it between his fingers, and stuck it behind his ear. He sucked the phlegm from his nose and spit it out. He patted his stomach and gave Henry a thumbs-up and a skeletal grin, a gold tooth perched in his jaw. His mouth moved: *Won't be long now.*

Gunny moved among them in an eccentric amble, touching them, addressing them as if they were schoolboys headed off to their first recital. Usually fearsome, in the chaos of the landing he was suddenly patient and caring.

"When you hit the beach do not stop," he said. "Do not crawl; roll. Do not fire over; fire around. Fire from different positions behind your cover. Move those ammo pouches so you can get closer to the ground if you need to. You defend yourself by attacking." He paused. "Try not to shoot yourself and do not shoot each other."

Henry was a hunter and Lew Devine was a hunter. This they shared as marines, but that was all Henry knew of him. Lew Devine was older and did not make friends. He'd fought in the Pacific, bloody Tarawa, Okinawa, the Solomons, where they stood back to back with one imperative: to hold the god damn position or die.

Lew Devine could sit still and quiet longer than any of them. He could slow his breathing and his pulse, and the exhalations of his breath and his heartbeat became almost imperceptible. He chewed gum constantly and there was a roll of white scar tissue where his right eyebrow should have been. Lew had been sick for most of the three weeks at sea as they waited offshore for the minesweepers and the frogmen to do their work. He'd lost fifteen pounds and wore his dungarees gathered at his skinny waist.

Lew uncapped his canteen. He leaned forward, bowed his head, and tipped the drink into his mouth.

"That's a good drink," he said to no one in particular.

"Water?" Henry said.

"Yes. Water."

The stiffness in Henry's legs began to melt away. Beneath his feet he could feel the vibrations of the mysterious and he felt to have traveled the eternal, circling half the world to reach the point that was this place in his life. For some seconds he thought of his mother, her beauty and grace, and his heart ached for her and he wished he'd been a better son.

When it was their turn to go, one man fell from the nets and went into the water and disappeared under the weight of his gear. He could not be saved. Another man's leg was crushed when he stepped between the scraping hulls. No sound could be heard coming from him, just the yaw of his open mouth as he screamed in agony, his boot torn away, and the crushed leg of his dungarees ragged and soaked with his blood.

They crossed the treacherous harbor through a luminous

mist and behind them was the apex of their widely spreading wake, the beacon lights reflecting on the swimming motes that densed in the wet sky. The lights bore through the thick air so powerfully they crackled in the ruptured atmosphere. Henry half closed his eyes to see better. What wandering current had he entered?

The coxswain's neck was stiff and bent back on his folded shoulders as he sought their designation for making land. There was a deafening explosion off the starboard and then they were drenched with seawater and debris, human and otherwise. The work of the frogmen and the minesweepers had not been perfect.

The coxswain laid off but then, finding their smoke, veered to starboard and then port. They bucked the white breakers and the dodging tide and then he caught the breakwater and gunned the engine, leaving behind them a muddy guttering wake slick with fuel and the air filled with gouts of black exhaust. At the last instant the coxswain backed off, reversing the engine, and it gnashed as the gears reknit.

When they punched onto Blue Beach and Henry stepped off, it was only to stumble and fall to his knees on the mudded and cobbled shore. They'd not been on land for almost three weeks and their legs were no longer quick enough to meet the hard rising earth. He strained under the heavy load that weighed his body. He carried a haversack, knapsack, cartridge belt, bayonet with scabbard, meat can with cover, knife-fork-spoon, canteen with cup and cover, first-aid packet and pouch, poncho, shelter half, steel helmet with liner, helmet cover, gas mask, entrenching tool, and grenade pouch.

He carried the BAR and two harnesses of .30-caliber magazines. He wore the .45 in a shoulder holster that belonged to his old uncle and the sheath knife that was also his uncle's. The BAR alone weighed twenty pounds and had a range of fifty-five hundred yards, more than three miles. Men debated whether or not you could kill a man at that distance or if he just disappeared over the curvature of the earth.

Gunny was running with them and then was down among them as they groaned and scrambled to their feet bearing the heavy weight of their armamentary. Gunny was tall and square built and born in 1905. He had been a marine since the age of sixteen and he was now forty-five years old and wore a long handlebar mustache he waxed every morning. He was now ferocious and screaming and cursing and kicking them in the ass.

"Get up, god dammit. Get up," he screamed.

"I'm trying," the man said.

"Quit your bitchin'," he barked. "You volunteered for this lash-up."

Gunny had told them that in battle one saw better and heard better and the body acted more quickly. The mind concentrated in battle. Old ailments and nagging injuries cleared up and in this way battle was very good for one's health. Henry collected himself and stood erect and stumbled and fell again, but he was not afraid. The possibility of being afraid was only an idea to him and had not yet entered into his mind. Though he agonized for the immense weight he felt entering his legs and hips, his heart beat like strong machinery and he plodded forward on feet and knees and feet.

"Good Lord," Lew kept saying, his words sawing the noise stricken air. "Good Lord," he cried as they staggered on their wobbly legs.

They scaled the fifteen-foot seawall on ladders to find a city disappeared in a pall of smoke and a veil of fog and dust eerily lit by fires burning on the distant landscape. The beacons jammed into the blown mess and stirred it like a wind. Overhead, the gull-winged dark blue Corsairs ripped the air, their .50-caliber guns silent as the amtracs dropped their tailgates and more men and machines and weapons entered the chaos and the equipment of war began to mass: jeeps, trucks, artillery, tanks, tractors, men. Hundreds of men in front of him and thousands behind him, and every fourth one of them screaming to be heard above the roar of the diesels belching black smoke, the clank of steel treads, the thousands of cogs, belts, cleats, tracks, pistons, and shivering cylinders exploding fuel, the yelling; the yelling slowly gave and inside all that noise he could hear a military band strike up to play.

"We are the most fortunate men," Henry said as he got his shoulder inside Lew's to help him over the wall. That was what the colonel had told them. They were the most fortunate men, because most times professional soldiers have to wait twenty-five years for another god damn war, but here they were with only five years wait for this one. He told them they would all be home by Christmas.

"It's a shitty deal. That's all I'm saying," Lew said.

"Quit your bitching or I am going to slap your jaw," Gunny said as he pushed by, a .45 clasped in his hand.

"He's a big operator, that one," Lew said.

"Fortunate, I say."

Henry looked at the black ocean behind him. Between his shoulder blades chafed a new tattoo, a blue and gray compass.

Three months ago he signed up and they immediately put him in the hospital. When his head wound had healed, they taught him commando, sniper, tommy gun, and BAR. They taught him stream, swamp, river, desert, and mountain. They taught him compass and first aid. They gave him three meals a day and a roof over his head, and he fired his rifle and screamed and bayoneted straw dummies. They told him he would be one of them forever.

He took one last look homeward the thousands of miles away, a ragged and empty wind, the verdigris light like burning copper in the quivering air. He knew he'd finally entered the enormity of existence, the sphere of the incredible.

.

Chapter 14

IT WAS THE KOREAN autumn when the division marched north through the dusty barren countryside, marched up through the rice fields and apple orchards. It was the shineless autumn sky in the season of mortality and turning into winter as they marched north along the east coast highway through the tiny villages. The fruit trees were leafless and stripped bare of their fruit and some were split and shivved and splintered with bullets and their upturned roots exploded from below the ground in broken claws.

They left the port that very day and they followed the colors north, the blue diamond, the scarlet and gold guidon, the stars and stripes. They crossed the hot plains, passing by fire-gutted warehouses and exploded factories, the nature of their industry made indecipherable for the work of the Corsairs and the distant naval guns. So complete was their work, Henry thought, perhaps it wasn't that at all. Perhaps they were factories in the production of smashed brick, tangled wire cable, contorted and twisted steel machinery. Perhaps this strange land manufactured bent and fire-scarred lathes; perhaps it peeled barrels, shredded motors, and violently dismantled substations.

They passed a little girl in a red plaid skirt and white blouse. She was wearing gray knee socks and white saddle shoes. She stood among burned timbers, crumbled bricks, and ruptured antitank mounts. She wore her school bag hiked over her thin shoulder and her black hair tied in a ponytail. She picked a stem of dry grass and offered it to him, and when he accepted it she smiled and plucked another for herself and placed the end in her white teeth.

They passed an old woman begging for food, her out-stretched hands purple and arthritic, an old man beside her wearing a black top hat and flowing white robe. He was lean-ing on a staff and his beard was so long he wore it tucked under his belt. The old man had only one foot and in the calmness of his face was the news that they were not the first foreign army he'd seen march in his life.

Everywhere there were small rectangular American and Korean flags on strawlike stems and there were swallows dis-appearing into a riverbank; and houses, their roofs thatched and the walls made of mud plastered to bundles of cornstalks and sorghum; an ox raised on scant feed pulling a wooden plow. There was a man with his dead strapped to his back, his head bowed with grief and a little boy walking beside him, his back crooked and his body bent to a crutch.

For a while there were children among them and nobody knew where they came from and then they disappeared.

It was a land of wood, hay, and stubble, a land as if he'd dreamt it, and he could not yet tell that these were the wit-nessings a man never forgets. He would remember it all in random unbidden moments and they would spring on him, and these would be among his occupying memories for the rest of his natural life.

They pushed north in parallel columns along both sides of the road toward Hamhung forty miles distant from the landing. Korean laborers bearing packed A-frames walked an interior line of march. They bore food and ammunition, batteries and medical supplies, wire and needles. After three weeks aboard the LSTs everyone's legs were weak and their bodies racked with flu. The sun was hot on the plains and many of the men passed out under their heavy loads and were picked up by shuttling jeeps and taken to the aid stations.

Lew was marching in front of Henry when suddenly he turned around and was marching backward. His body was squat and thickly muscled, but he had a high-fluting voice and sounded more like a girl than a man when he spoke. His hair was red and flat, and more out of habit than vanity he combed it every chance he could. He smiled; his gold tooth flashed.

He told Henry he was from Charleston and wanted to know where Henry was from.

"Charleston," Henry told him.

"Charleston, West Virginia," Lew clarified.

"The same," Henry said.

"Someone tol' me that," Lew said, and snapped about.

Another mile and he turned backward again. He told Henry he'd been in the Pacific and joined up again because he wanted to buy a persimmon yellow Jaguar automobile and have it shipped from England to America. His mother was a widow, and if he died instead of lived, she would have the money he was saving for his Jaguar automobile and she would also be the beneficiary of his National Service Life Insurance Policy.

"Ten grand worth of Uncle Sam's money," he said. "She could use it. Not bad for a few months' work, either way you look at it. Of course, I'd have to be dead for her to make out. What about you?"

Henry smiled. "Before he died, my grandfather encouraged me to travel."

"The hell you say," Lew said, and looked at him queerly and then gave Henry a second look that he took to mean they would be friends.

"Maybe we'll be fortunate," Henry said.

"Quit your fucking around," Gunny said as he came back down the line.

"I hear that," Lew said, and gave a wink of his eye.

Lew turned about, and then he turned again after Gunny disappeared.

"Him and me were in the Pacific together. He's a real pussycat."

For a time they rode under canvas in trucks over the dusty and bumpy road, their tailbones bouncing on the hard wooden slats of the seats, their spines jarring against the rake of the sideboards. While some took pleasure in the truck rides, their grinding transmissions, roaring engines, and stinking exhausts, the trucks fatigued Henry and he wanted to be marching again. After being at sea for so long, he wanted to be moving on his own two feet.

Their progress slowed as they encountered clusters of

Korean families moving south. A marine reached out from the back of the truck with his lit cigarette and set slow fire to a mattress bundled atop an A-frame a Korean was carrying. The men in the truck laughed and then a second marine, imitating the first, did the same, lighting fire to a family's bedding perched on an A-frame. Henry wanted to say something for how wrong that was, but he didn't. He looked to Lew who didn't say anything either. He knew the violence that seemed to be always within them, convulsive and necessary. Daily, there were fistfights on the transports for slights real or perceived.

"You shouldn't ought to do that," Henry said, and the men quieted.

"What the fuck does it matter to you?" the first marine said, turning his attention, rising up over him.

Henry covered his eyes with his hands, paused, and then stood up to confront the man.

"Leave him alone," Lew said. "He's just a kid."

"There's no need to go sticking your oar in," the marine said, but clearly he did not want to get into it with Lew. Henry sat back down.

"You missed a great opportunity to keep your mouth shut," Lew said.

Lew's words stung, but they were enough to save him a beating and the soldier backed away as the drivers let out the clutches one after another and their engines revved, the trucks lurching forward. They were on the move again and then their truck jumped and stalled out and the driver was roundly mocked.

The truck was moving ahead, but not long before it stopped and let them out for no reason they could see. They were in another nowhere place just a few miles beyond the nowhere place they'd recently left behind.

"Right about now I wish I was anywhere but here," Lew said.

"Where would you go?" Henry asked.

"Anywhere is good enough."

"Mount up!" Gunny bawled out.

"He's a corker, that one," Lew said, and they stepped off and they were marching again on both sides of the road humping north to where they did not know. There was a deep ditch that ran alongside the road, and as Henry walked he scrutinized it for cover on a moment's notice and then conceded each found place to the next man in the marching line and found another. He kept walking that he might inherit the next sanctuary of deadfall or boulder, a copse of scrub pine.

The confrontation in the truck, he let it pass from his mind. However right he'd been, he felt a boy and a foolish boy for having spoken up, but what else could he have done?

He came to a place beneath hackled trees where Lew was looking at something. Three men and a woman lay in the ditch. Theirs were heads without backs to them, their hands bound with wire. They were his first dead. Their faces were blown and contorted and he thought what hard painful work to be killed.

"Don't think about it," Lew said.

"When do the hunters go up?"

"When they need us."

"When will that be?" Henry said.

"Not ever, I hope."

He passed from beneath the hackled trees and the high wind of autumn was roaring overhead. He remembered seeing the compass rose on his back, the image traveling from the mirror held up behind to the mirror he held in his hands. He touched at his pocket where letters were collected and then he walked on, a hitch in his step on the side where lay the heavy weight of his weapon.

Chapter 15

THEY MARCHED DEEPER INTO the north, deeper into the season, and it seemed with each step the air was changing, cooling, closing its grasp on the earth. In the days to come it would sharpen and feel good and then turn brittle and sugar with frost and freeze and become deadly.

Yesterday, he'd seen kids playing marbles on the grounds of an abandoned elementary school.

The soldiers they were driving north were hungry and tired and murderous. There were more ditches, more of the murdered and executed, their wired hands, their blown heads. To the south, from where they came, there were reports of bandits raiding the supply lines. The word went out the Chinese had entered the war, men had been bayoneted in their sleeping bags, and to the west was a three-day running battle, fighting man to man, hand to hand, and fifteen hundred enemy killed. Each new arrival was inspected and questioned for news of his experience; each had heard the stories too or knew someone who had, but they seemed impossible stories: they were going to drop the bomb, they'd be home for Christmas. Lew half believed it to be so. In fact, he half believed everything he heard.

Henry walked on, erect under the drag of his pack and the weight of the BAR. For him these stories were the whisperings of fate, the undertow of inevitability, and nothing could change where he stood. His grandfather had fought in the war between the states. His uncles in Mexico and France. They tamed horses and they rode them. They'd put their hands on horses every single day of their lives and they thought the horse was God's finest creature, finer than God himself, and he'd been trained at their knees that soldiering was work and this was the work his family did. He did not worry it and he trusted he would be good at it when the time came.

They spent that night in Hamhung, where they cleaned their rifles and ate spaghetti, mashed potatoes, lettuce, and cake and lay down in a dirty warehouse under a corrugated steel roof that heated by day with the ever-slanting sun. In sunlight it became like a griddle on a stove, crumpling and banging with expansion and now with the cool night it pinged with contraction. The warehouse floor was gritted with iron filings and scattered steel shavings and held by years of seeping oil from leaking machines. All the machinery was gone. All the copper was stripped from the walls and not a bolt or a screw left behind. In the warehouse he found a child's toy and articles of clothing.

The hunters, Henry and Lew among them, kept to themselves in their own corner of the vast shed and would continue to do so wherever they billeted: the little schools, the halls and churches. They kept their own fires and their own mess. They were, for the most, unmarried and childless men.

They ate together and slept together. Each knew where the other was at all times. To say they were outcasts would be inaccurate, and to say they were hard men would be wrong because some of them were only boys but boys who were already men. When it was their turn, when those who had gone before the column were dead or fatigued, they'd step up and they would take the point and like the videttes of old, they would be first up the road.

They lay awake that night with their backs to the walls or sprawled on their sleeping bags. Lew showed him a brightly colored Hawaiian shirt, his one item of person he intended to wear whenever he needed cheering up.

"Do you know the one about Prince Albert in the can?" one of them said.

"Hey, fathead," Lew said. "Shut the fuck up."

"Lew, you're such a son of a bitch," the one said.

In the darkness there were long rows of floating cigarette embers until one by one they went out, and they fell asleep for how tired they were. Soon the rats came out and chewed at their bootlaces and sipped the peach syrup from ration cans. The rats found jelly beans and held them in their paws and ate them as if they were small oblong heads. The rats sat on their chests, licking the syrup from their paws, and crawled across their sleeping faces and suddenly one man woke up cursing and another man woke up and fired a .38 into the darkness. The gunshot cracked and echoed in the high hollow chamber of the warehouse, causing every man to come from sleep, grab and charge a weapon. When the warehouse lighted with the hissing white glare of lanterns, it was an illuminated tableau of lethal men crouched on their knees, curled close to the floor like animals and no more than a length of breath from exploding.

But no one else fired his weapon, and with the single round nothing was killed or wounded. There was no threat for the moment, so they laughed it off and unstrung themselves and settled down again, but Henry's heart beat painfully in his chest. His veins, neck, and eyes strained and pulsed. Killing rats, he realized, was another way in which you could be killed.

In the morning he awoke to graying in the east. The order went out to shave so they heated water and took out their soap and razors, and their cheeks were newly blue in the morning's cold. In the still-gray dawn the wind picked up and there was the clang of corrugated metal from the roof. It was a cloudy cold sky, slate blue, with a strange halo around the sun.

That day they continued north through a wooded valley with trees on both sides of the road. They carried their weapons in the crooks of their arms or yoked across their shoulders. In their slouching stride they could walk all day and all night. On the air was the scent of pine trees and running in the deep shadows there was a thin stream with frozen moss, jeweled green and blue with glittering melt ice. Then the countryside thinned of life and opened up again and the cold began to promise discomfort.

His walking dream was to awake some day soon and it be a hot and musty room in the boathouse, folded in the satin heat of the city, the flat black river flowing beneath the bed, the sound of the rattling train from over river. Mercy's back is naked and she's sitting on the edge of the bed brushing her hair.

"Don't it hurt," he says.

"I like it," she says, collecting and balling the hair from the bristles.

"I can do it for you," he says, and she hands him the brush.

"Tonight," she says, "you come see me?"

"I don't know," he says, drawing the brush through her hair.

"You better," she says, "or I will come find you and kick down the door."

Beneath them the play of water, a slap and gulp in the eddies that swirled about the pilings, the big fish sounding.

He wrote and rewrote words in his mind. *Dearest Mercy . . . Where are you? . . . I am here and the knowing part of me tells me why . . . Tonight I think I was on my way here all along and have now arrived . . . As much as I want to let go of the past, that cannot be. I am held by the recent memory of . . .*

He'd experienced little, but what he'd experienced with Mercy he'd experienced the all of it. He wanted to believe it again, but she'd disappeared, and try as he might, he could not. He wrote to forget as much as to remember.

He marched on, silently. She was with him now, through tight passes on the road that followed a rock-strewn riverbed where tufted willows grew, and then she was gone.

In some steps came the distinct sensation he'd been here before and had remained in some formless shape that was waiting for him to resume his presence, and now he was stepping inside and the shape was fitting him. The shape rose up from the earth or descended from the sky and closed about him. The fit was uncanny and frightening. This was home now and these men were his true family. His grandfather had told him that in war most of the time you only remember what happens six feet to either side of you, so he continued to map every new landmark and identify every new strongpoint.

To the east there was a triangle of locust trees all bent in the same direction as if they'd raised themselves in a constant wind. To the west was a mountain peak that rose to height in staggered elevations so perfectly structured it might be the constructed burial mound for a giant race of people. There, an odd shelf of rock resting in opposition to the prevailing syncline. But on the whole, it was an empty and barren country, and clouds were banking. It was colder now and there would be a snow.

They advanced farther up the road, deeper into the country. Spotter planes were constantly leaving from the east and returning from the west, drifting, circling, floating. The line of march was already too long and too thin to be supplied and supported by reinforcements, and they all knew this, even the fools among them. Each man knew they were the lethal plaything of the old men who directed them, the old men who were always fighting the last war.

He knew they'd be coming back down this road, and when they did he knew they'd be cold and hungry, winnowed and bleeding. It was just a matter of time.

"Henry," Lew called, whipping around smartly to march

backward. "What's the story about the kids leave bread crumbs in the woods to find their way back?"

"How should I know?" he said.

"You're a kid, ain't you?"

"I don't 'member."

"How old are you?"

"Old enough."

"My mind has to know what that damn story is."

"One of us will 'member," Henry said, and Lew spun forward again.

Loose stones grated under his boot treads. No matter how he tried not to, he thought of Mercy and when he did she was always inside a shroud of mystery. Their days together were silent or spent talking about nothing at all. He held memory of kissing her and their lovemaking in the white and gold rooms, desperate and hungry for each other. They preyed on each other and tore deeply and always left behind was a small emptiness that needed to be filled again. There were times now when he hated her, but it was hatred short lived. It would flash in his mind and burn brightly and disappear in a wondering question. Where did she go?

"Hansel and Gretel," he whispered, remembering the time before this time.

Chapter 16

I N THE MORNING SLEEPING bags hung from every tree, drying after a night's cold and bitter drizzle. Snow had fallen in the night, the temperature had plummeted, and all about them was the cracking rime. He wondered if daylight would come at all and then it did. It was still snowing, great heavy flakes as large as wood shavings.

The stink of burning diesel fuel permeated the air as the heavy engines built to a din. They ate pancakes with syrup and drank scalding-hot coffee and after breakfast they drew on cold-weather gear: pile-lined parkas with fur-trimmed hoods, mittens with trigger fingers, mitten inserts, waterproof trousers, clumsy thermo boots, heavy socks.

They'd given up their steel helmets and they wore Korean caps made of dog fur with ear lappets, one down and one up to hear and then change sides to warm the cold ear. The march north was fast and had not been foreseen and many of them lacked woolen underwear, parkas, and fur caps.

A game of football broke out and they tackled each other in the snow. They sweated and they shed their new gear and their thighs burned. One man dislocated his shoulder and another broke a finger. And then they were told to mount up.

That afternoon they filed past steel drums of boiling water and with long tongs a cook fished out cans of meat and beans for each. There was more scalding-hot coffee and tins of fruit cocktail. Their calves ached from the cold of the march. So swift were the events of the last few days, Henry could not recollect where he had been or what a time he'd had. One night he'd slept in a dog tent and another night in an abandoned warehouse and another on a goose-feather mattress in a half-destroyed house and another night they billeted in a disused church.

Higher still, they crossed the terrestrial ice of the freezing plain, the frost line, and pushed even higher as anxious to find its source. There was only cold and more cold. On one side was the Yellow Sea and on the other the Sea of Japan. It was a war-torn country, five hundred miles long and two hundred miles wide. When they reached the next plateau a blast of extreme cold was sweeping across the land and causing much suffering to the sparse population and would continue to do so through the teeth of that season.

They paused again. Stretched along the roadway were shacks made of lumber and concrete block. Daylight was a rapidly declining element as the sun hurried from the sky earlier each day. It would be colder than any cold he'd ever experienced in his life. When they stopped, they paced and beat their chests with their fists. They did not fall out in the ditches and along the berms because the sweat of march sapped their body heat, and sitting down to stand up again required more effort than worth sparing. It became as if a single electric nerve ran through them. It diminished their hunger and tightened the muscles in their shoulders. It clarified their vision and made their hearing more acute. It coursed beneath their thinking minds and for some it became their minds and washed away the thoughts of all other possibilities in the world of life except cold.

They marched on and as they marched there was the singularity of them, the short-time self-sufficiency of men laden with war gear walking a mountain road in a foreign land. As Henry climbed the road, it was as if he were held aloft on the palm of a great outstretched hand buffeted by cold and wind, a bringer of death. Canteens began to ice and freeze and split. Bolts froze in the weapons. There were hobbling men with blackened toes inside their boots and hands cracking open with chilblains.

The numbers of the Korean laborers began to dwindle, and the farther north they pushed they melted into the countryside. Men with short time left to serve began to lag or hide in caves until they could hitch a ride to the rear and the sea and home.

Lew turned around to walk backward against the snow stinging like shot pellets. He held out his canteen and Henry took a drink. His body shook for the solution of water, grapefruit juice, and the sick-bay alcohol it contained.

"That's candy for you," Lew said, and then he said, "This fucking road's getting longer all the time." His remark traveled backward and forward and across the road and continued until it returned to him and he agreed with silent assent as if it were a true spoken wisdom.

"Something is out there," Henry said.

"No shit, Sherlock."

"Devine," Gunny growled, and Lew turned back around.

It was then a man, a ragged Korean soldier, passed south through the middle of their column. He stared in concentration at the space just before him where in seconds his body would be. His face held no expression but was scraped off on one side and on the other side his head shaved and bandaged. In a little while, there was another, unarmed and wounded in no apparent way, but similarly stared out in front as if a pilgrim inexplicably denied and sent back to his former life.

"The little cocksuckers," someone said, and a grumbling coursed the line.

Then they were coming in a silent, determined stream and there was no more judgment from the marines. Coming down from the north were ranks of the bloodied and they passed through them, some shoeless and their feet black and making a clacking sound as they walked, and yet they kept marching in the direction of the long distant harbor. Some collapsed and fell in the road, staining it with their blood, and an aid station was established alongside the road dispensing blood, water, and morphine and then continuing them on their southern migration.

Henry stopped at a waterfall frozen into a great blue stalk where the milky water had turned to ice and men set a fire and broke ice to melt in an iron kettle. They added their own wood, boards, boxes, and pallets to the fire and dipped their tin cups into the kettle and held them under the melting icicles and took long drinks.

"This is real pretty," one of them said.

"Dream on," Lew said, knocking his cup against his rifle butt.

"Mind if I have a little?" Henry said, stepping up with his cup.

"Yeah, knock yourself out," the one said. He drank the cold water from the blue fall and then moved on so the next man could drink.

All day long was to be experienced the dead weight of waiting as hour after hour they walked the hard road, waiting for the enemy who were invisible and yet seemed to be so many they were stirring the air itself. Still, no one saw them, but he knew they were out there.

That night the setting sun shed a cold bluish twilight over the land and the evening sky was cloudless and metallic. Lew produced a bottle of Old Overholt whisky and he had a pull. They passed it around their circle, the skewed faces of the men in the light of the burning fire. Each had a drink and then they had another and continued until the bottle was empty and then tried to get a few hours sleep.

In his pocket Henry carried Tootsie Rolls and a letter from his mother. He'd been carrying the letter for how many days he did not know. He slit the seal with his knife. The penmanship was from a hand as if learning to write. Her letter began, *It's four thirty here, and where you are your day is just beginning. I would be grateful to have some word from you.*

It was all he could read. He refolded the letter and slipped it back inside its envelope. He knew he should read it, knew he should write to her, but for some reason he could not bring himself to do these things. He carefully unfolded the letter and read again, *Thank you again for this address. I cannot say I was surprised. You boys are the heirs of men and their inheritance is yours . . . Beware the snares of the evil one. May the love of the angels hold you inside their wings.*

He began to compose a letter in his mind: *I am in the field, somewhere in Korea, north of the thirty-eighth parallel. You are in my thoughts and in my heart . . .* But he could not go on. He did not want to be loved, did not want to be remembered, and then sleep overtook him.

Chapter 17

THE NEXT MORNING WHEN Henry awoke he lay under a foot of newly fallen snow. The trucks were revving up, but he could not see them or reach them to warm by their engines. He sat up and brushed the snow aside and realized he was the first to awake. He watched as each man came into the shock of the day. One by one they sat up and looked about. Their faces were those of helpless, ghostly children. They rubbed their eyes and stretched their arms and rolled over to stand upright in their wool underwear. It was as if each were reluctantly coming from his own private death to regretfully be born into life again.

Henry stomped his feet in a clumsy dance and pounded his arms to his chest. His breath was white puffs of steam that quickly froze on his face and the chest of his parka.

Lew hawked a gob of phlegm into his mittened hand and studied it. Someone said it was ten degrees and it was enough to start an occupying argument. An icy red glow flared in the southeast and the frozen and shuttered land became a profile of multiplicated spurs, razors, and spines many times folded.

"Please kill me," Lew said.

"You know I can't do that," Henry said.

"You got a cig?"

Henry squeezed one from his pack and lit it. He rubbed his hands together and then he cupped a hand and lit one for himself. They drew quietly on their cigarettes, the smoke steely in their mouths.

"What do you think is up there?"

"I don't know," Lew said. "Nothing good."

"I wish I knew."

"The enemy don't hardly ever cooperate the way they should."

After his smoke Lew diagnosed himself sick and went to stand in line where he tipped back his head to receive aspirin pills and a solution of water and sick-bay alcohol. When he returned he told Henry he found the experience so restorative he got back in line three more times. While waiting, he had the opportunity to slick a large can of pineapple juice and this they shared.

There was also mail. Lew received a letter from his mother and Henry received another letter from his.

I am sitting at the kitchen table. There is no word from Mercy though I do not travel in those circles. Your man Walter came by the other day. He said to tell you he sold the horse upcountry as well as the rest of them. He said you'd know which one. He is moving to the state of Florida and needed the money. He said he sold ever thing before the bank could close on him. He said you would know which horse and he trusted you would understand . . . Last night you came to me in a dream . . .

I have seen your fate and it is not there and the light was
not dark. You will learn what you need to know. You
will return to me. That's all I know and this morning I am
so relieved.

It was the most he could endure to read. Hers was a world
of certainty and providence. She did not believe in accident.
And he wondered on the Gaylen horse and where she might
be. He had the passing thought he'd find her when he got
home and buy her for himself.

He worked down through the layers of clothing and put
the letter in a breast pocket with the others.

That day there was turkey with all the trimmings, cranberry sauce, and giblet gravy and it all froze after a few bites.

"I don't want no damn turkey," Henry said.

"What's the matter, ain't you hungry," Lew said, hacking
away at his plate.

"Who could eat that? It's all frozen as soon as it hits your
plate."

"You don't like Thanksgiving?"

"We just never made much of it."

"Ain't you American? What's wrong with you?"

"I was thinking, Lew, I have never killed anyone. There
ain't no practice for something like that."

"You'll be okay."

"How can you tell?"

"You're a funny one," Lew said.

"I'll just trust you can tell."

While the others ate, Henry found a grinding wheel in an

abandoned barn and for some hours he worked the treadle, sharpening bayonets and fighting knives, the skree of the blades, a rooster tail of sparks, as the wind swirled around them.

Over the skree of the turning wheel, Lew told them about Borneo, or was it New Guinea? He was asleep in his tent one night and thought a Japanese soldier had snuck in and was going to kill him with a knife. But it was a gorilla snuck into his tent and it beat the living hell out of him. In the morning he was all black and blue.

The sound made by the steel and stone was like a song to Henry and he did not mind as more and more men stood by quietly with their bayonets and personal knives for him to do his work.

"Take these. I'm afraid they'll get me today." It was a marine standing by his side, holding a packet of letters, attempting to shove them into his hands. The marine was on suicide watch as he'd accidentally shot another marine.

"Why are you giving them to me?" Henry said.

"They'll never get you. I can tell."

"What can you tell?" he said. It was the same as Lew told him not two hours ago.

"They won't get you," the marine said.

"I don't want your letters," Henry said. "I got my own to carry."

"That guy is bananas," Lew said. "Don't get personal," he said. "These guys are a bunch of ignoramuses."

Lew gave to him a handful of dollar bills, the sum he'd been charging men to have Henry sharpen their blades.

They climbed again that afternoon, the valley long distant and entered the high snow-covered mountains. The road passed abandoned huts and thick belts of stunted pine. Where before the people had come to the roadside to beg for food, they'd now disappeared. Pushed down from the heights were tiny deer. They ran down the center of the column and wove among the jeeps and trucks, their hooves clicking on the stony road and then skittered down the off side.

The wind blew like a scythe, but they kept north, crossing another plateau and marching up the road. It was an empty and evermore desolate country they entered, a landscape of stunted evergreen, granite boulders, and swirling winds of snow.

On the road that day he saw a large lumber pile in the center of a field, farmhouses in a small valley, old tires mounted on their roofs to keep them in place. He saw a dead boy he took to be no more than fourteen. The boy's face stared up at him. The look was mild, even peaceful, bored, and innocent. The look was nothing at all and as if the face had yet to be placed on the head of a man to lead him into life.

In the evening the western sky lit scarlet and the call went out for them. It was their turn. They would now work ahead of the moving column and their time would be the loneliest time in the world.

Gunny moved among them. He put his hands on each as he spoke to their assembly.

"Do not get in a fight," he said. "Go patiently. Don't go far. See what you can see and let us know what you see. Keep your mouth shut and listen. You can hear pretty well at forty below zero. Do not get in a fight. That's not your job. If you do get in a fight, do not get killed."

"When do we go?" Lew said.

"You go now," Gunny told him, placing his hands on Lew's shoulders.

"What's the point of being born?" Lew said. "I have never understood."

"You're a real wise guy," Gunny said, his somber face never seeming to smile.

Henry swapped off the BAR for a carbine he cradled across his chest. Rigged out with lightened packs, one after another they stepped off. They passed through the ranks of men eating and fallen out and the ranks of men who themselves had been in the lead and they entered the night. If there was anything more to know, no one told them.

Lew went first and Henry was second with the others following. They staggered their departures and strung out along the evening road, somehow warmer at night, with enough space between them so that a shell or a machine gun would kill only one of them. Lew said the hunters were often allowed to pass unharmed. Lucky for them, but hell for the rest, so they were to keep their wits about them.

That night there was a stillness in the sky. Day had been transformed into night and a blue light was resting on the land down to the orange banks of a frozen river. Henry walked on, more quickly than advised, hoping to catch a glimpse of Lew out ahead, and then he slowed and in the hours to come he followed as ordered. At times the road disappeared in snow and the wind made shadowy figures and he could have walked off the edge if not careful, and at other times the night was still and the road was swept clean, its gravel surface sparkling with moonlight. That was the beauty and the terror of this world and he was alone in it.

Rounding a bend in the mountain he saw a man standing in the road. It was Lew smoking a cigarette while looking at something. He stopped and they stood together at an overlook.

"Look at this," Lew said, and there were hundreds of footprints in the snow coming from the offside, crossing the road and ascending the mountain.

They turned to stand with their backs pressed tight against each other. The wind was getting up again, chasing away the footprints and all around them the environing cold and snow and darkness.

"What kind of pie do you like best?" Lew said.

"Apple."

"I like berry pies."

"Any particular kind?" Henry said, the darkness so close to his face he could feel it. He watched down the road for sight of the man who trailed him.

"I like all berries and rhubarb too."

"Rhubarb's good."

Henry allowed himself a glance over the precipice. There were jagged rocks thirty feet below and beyond them a steep drop down a cliff and below that was only darkness. He could not understand how anyone came up that side, let alone hundreds of men.

"I do not like this moment," Lew said.

"What was it like in the Pacific?" Henry said.

"You do not want to know."

"Something's going to happen."

"Nothing happens until it happens."

The wind crossing their open position made all talk seem as if it were a constant chant. He let more of his weight against Lew's back and felt a propping weight returned.

"What are you thinking now," Lew said, the words the need to keep talking.

"I never thought hell would be so cold."

They stood aslant as the canalized wind blew about them, sharp as hunger. From the peaks and into the valleys the wind whooped and roared.

"You want to know what it's like?" Lew said.

"I do."

"You save the last bullet for yourself. I know one thing," Lew said.

"What?"

"When I get home I am going to eat a berry pie as big as a woman's ass."

The wind blew and was like a blade to their bodies. Henry caught sight of the man trailing him. He turned and Lew stood erect and together they kept north, crossing the plateau.

In the morning they'd report they'd seen nothing except hundreds of footprints in the snow. They'd breakfast on hamburger patties, fruit cocktail, and jelly beans and he'd be shocked how restorative a little food and water. One of them would not unfasten his brass roller belt buckle fast enough and he'd half piss himself and be ridiculed for it. Then they'd climb into a truck to get some sleep as it lumbered up the road. His body would shake with its rewarming and it'd be a nice way to end the day, the emptiness in his heart.

As he walked he again saw his mother in her vegetable garden among the husking corn and frosted tomatoes, that time of the brittle and the dying. He wondered if he'd ever live to be a remembering man like his grandfather and his uncles, the kind of man who when old and tired sat in the dim light of fire and let his mind span the years and well up with the water of memory.

Chapter 18

O N THOSE BLACK NIGHTS, strung along the frozen road, there were two stories in his mind, the story of then and the story of the unfolding now.

In his mind he wrote to her. *Dear Mercy, all the tears in the world cannot cry enough for how much I miss you. Our days together were like a dream inside a dream inside a dream . . .* And his mind papered with an account of the sadness and confusion and the deep mysterious event that they'd been.

There were whole days when he could not now remember what she looked like, but he remembered her hair, chestnut and fine and straight and sometimes she wore it knotted at the back of her head, how her long bangs strayed across her forehead, masking her ivory face and eyes so bright. It was as though he dreamed that season. He fought for the memory of her. It was coming to him from far away. He stretched out his hand to touch the image as if it was not in his mind but standing before him. The image remained.

"Am I really touching you," he whispered. He stopped walking and touched his cold mittened hand to his own forehead. He tried to remember the tilt of her hips, her warm kisses, her trailing fingers. He knew you can only understand things after they've happened, but try as he might, he could not understand what happened and that told him it must still be happening and suddenly he was crushed by her memory.

After the image faded it was again okay if he got killed. He would not have minded.

He climbed to where the road bottlenecked in a steep narrow pass forty-seven hundred feet high. At that elevation there were no forks in the road, just one steep side and the other steeper side, the winds slicing down from the north.

Lew came from the rocks, came up behind him before he knew it. He'd managed to light a cigarette inside the cover of his fur-lined hood.

"We will have to hold this pass," he said.

Henry squinted and nodded his head. What Lew meant was they would have to hold this pass or they would be trapped and every man of them killed. Already their advance was way beyond any thought for the future.

"Maybe she wasn't the one for you," Lew said, finishing his cigarette and letting the wind strip it away.

"Who?"

"Whoever it is those letters remind you of."

Henry knew there was nothing there to hold on to with Mercy, nothing that had lasted more than a hot season and yet he wanted that day to return when they were together. He knew she held some unknown part of him.

"When you fall in love with a woman," Lew said, "it's over for you and you might's well die."

Lew told him he was engaged to three women: Bernadette,

Viv, and Kitty. All three of them were lovelies and were waiting for him. He then said in no uncertain terms that Henry needed to get his head out of his ass.

On the twisting road behind them was the division and on the other side of the pass was a descent into the five-fingered valley of Yudam-ni, a little village tucked in the foothills of the high peaks of the Taebeks, the frozen Yalu River, Manchuria.

"This is about the last place I can think of I'd like to get hurt bad," Lew said.

"Which way?" Henry said.

"It don't matter," Lew said. "There's no right way to do a wrong thing." He paused. "That way," he finally said with a chop of his hand.

The next night they rigged out and slipped into the darkness again, leaving behind the shallow scraped-out foxholes. Each man on line in snow and ice was looking across a field at a mountain, intent on some inner world as he listened to the eerie sounds the wind blew.

They took up a forward position on the flank of a high rugged spur on a ridge to the north. Gunny told them if there was an attack it would be at night to avoid the airships. He told them the enemy, who were not confirmed to be in country, moved and fought at night. They wore thick padded green or white uniforms, caps with a red star, carried a personal weapon, eighty rounds of ammunition, a few stick grenades, spare foot rags, sewing kit and a week's ration of fish, rice, and tea. Their day began at 7 p.m. They marched until 3 a.m. and then prepared camouflaged positions for the day. Only scouts moved in daylight. It would be close and mixed up. They'd get inside the mortars. They would rush past, trying to get as deep into their position as possible, and attack the command posts. They would probe the weaknesses, swarm and divide and isolate and then kill one by one. It was their way of fighting. They cut off the head, he told them, and the body died. It was the way they'd won the Chinese war. Gunny knew because he'd been there and he admired them for how willing they were to die.

They tried to scrape the ground, digging to bury their profiles, but the earth underneath them was frozen over a foot deep and so finally they stretched out on a high shelf of earth, hunkered inside the green hoods of their parkas where they could watch and listen. On the mountain ridges there were four rifle battalions lying in darkness and behind them were battalions of artillery. To the northeast was a frozen reservoir.

The cold felt like a thousand needles cutting into his face and not a star was showing in the slatelike sky. As the hours of darkness passed, the cold sky cleared and blued and a ghostly moon appeared.

In his mind he traveled back to the city. He was supposed to be in school. He knew that he'd lived there but now could not remember having done so. He'd lied about his age at the recruitment office and they did not seem to care.

He recalled Lew's advice. He was changed since last night and it was as if a gift conferred.

A sound, what was it? He cocked his head and listened.

There were no sounds unknown. All sounds had source and were signature. It came again, the crunch of snow.

Someone was approaching, silent as a pulse beat. The sound stopped and slowly the sound back traced its path.

"I think we are in for a very uncertain future," Lew said. He lay beside him, a walkie-talkie inside his parka to keep it warm.

"They talk about you," Henry whispered.

"What do they say?"

"There is no one meaner or tougher than Lew Devine."

"Shit," Lew said, and spit.

"Do you think we'll ever get back home?"

"Not tonight."

"You know, Lew, they got names."

"I don't know their names," Lew said.

"It's easy enough to find out."

"I don't know their names because I don't want to know their names."

"You know mine."

"My cross to bear."

There was a stillness in the sky, the deep blue light resting on the land down to the shadowed blackness of the dry streambed and back up again and turning black as it silhouetted the parallel ridge. After a while Lew fell asleep, the black stubble of his frozen beard wreathed with ice, while Henry kept watch and it was some time later a deer materialized, stepping tenderly among the heaped boulders in the dry streambed. The deer was white and was not stepping as much as it was simply moving, as if passing in a world of

private ether. It only seemed aware of the great antlers it wore
on its head. This he concluded for how tilted its head, as if
threading the air, as if weaving its tines into the sky.

He scanned the black silhouette of the parallel ridge and
when he cut his eyes back to the streambed, the white deer
had disappeared and he was changed back and his heart was
filled with longing and fear. He stood watch the next hour on
a parapet, a stone ledge in their tiny redoubt. He let Lew sleep
on as the lonely light of a blue-gray mist was giving way and
steely night was falling and the world becoming a deeper and
deeper gloom. He blew on his curled red fingers and wiped
snot from his nose. The cold and fatigue made him gloomy
and simpleminded. This night is awful, he thought, but it is
still a night in my life. He felt pain and bitterness but also a
strange sweetness so complete as his worlds began to merge.
He just wanted to lie down and be still.

With the toe of his boot he nudged at Lew who came from
sleep instantly and in full possession of himself, his weapons
and his ability to use them. With his gloved hand he muffled
a cough and a gurgle and silently cleared his throat onto
the ice.

"Another crummy night in old Korea," he finally said.

"Great view," Henry said.

"That's why you woke me up?"

"Watch," Henry said, and for only an instant the earth
seemed to move, to take and hold a breath.

"Rest your eyes," Lew said, but he did not rest his eyes.

"I think we're outnumbered," he said.

When the morning light rose behind them, the mountain

shadows lifted and in the grim dawn the terrain before them was as if a vast and turbulent sea, successive ridge after successive ridge.

At daybreak there was a rumble in the east and suddenly the bombers were on station high overhead. Marine Corsairs ripped through the near atmosphere. Their fins were like steel knives cutting cold and in their wake they left invisible moils of air.

At breakfast there were rumors they were moving west again and linking up with Walker's Eighth Army. The word went out to mount up. The rumor confirmed, they were pushed west on the only road cutting through the great ridges of the looming mountains, but not for long. A spotter plane messaged there were road blocks in their path. The engineers moved up with flamethrowers and then diesel bulldozers and with their wide blades they shoved the charred debris aside and sent the stone and logs plummeting into the valley below.

They moved on again and came to a frozen stream and a stone bridge, the bottom a gorge of scouring creek boulder. They waited again for the engineers to blow more road blocks and the bulldozers to clear them away.

"The Reds are out there," Lew said. "I'd bet money on it and I'm not a gambling man." And then, "If you get killed by an enemy who is not there," Lew said, "are you then not dead?"

Henry suggested Lew take it up with the padre who wore a purple stole and carried a .38 in a shoulder holster. Lew said he just might do that and when he returned he said the padre suggested he quit his horseshit, do his job, and stop wasting the padre's time.

"He said that?" Henry asked.

"Not in so many words," Lew said, "but there was a lot of emotion behind them. I think the padre's gone a little mental."

"You'd have to start out a little mental to be him," Henry said. "Tell me again why we came up here and what we are looking for."

"Look what I got," Lew said, waggling a cigar between his fingers.

"Where'd you get that?"

"The padre," Lew said.

Lew cut the cigar, giving Henry half and keeping the other half for himself.

Chapter 19

THAT NIGHT, THE WIND-BLOWN snow an impenetrable veil, they rigged out and stepped off again. Darkness now came at four thirty and would last for sixteen hours. They passed through the front line and disappeared, entering the wilderness on the coldest and blackest of nights. They moved slowly, step by step, their bodies low and compressed, heel to toe, separating themselves from the men, the guns, the engines, the iron. They stopped and waited and listened and moved again.

"It won't be long now," Lew whispered.

"Are you not afraid?"

"Don't be afraid until there's something to be afraid of."

They occupied a rocky labyrinth of granite formations. Inside the frosted rocks it was smooth and cold and tomblike. Where they lay had never seen the sun or light or warmed on a summer day. Inside they found a sitting dead, his arms frozen in position to hold the rifle that someone had taken away from him. He wore a quilted coat and canvas rubber-soled shoes and was gray and rimed with frost and indistinguishable and like the rocks themselves.

"Last night," Henry whispered, "I saw something."

"What'd you see?" Lew said, feeding a stick of spearmint gum into his mouth.

"A deer. It was white."

"I saw it too," Lew said.

"What do you think it means?" Henry said.

"Don't be that way. Get some sleep."

Henry zipped his bag over his legs to his waist and flattened himself against the slant wall of their stone chamber. He tried to sleep a little and when he next looked at the luminous hands on his wristwatch he thought that he might have, but no time at all had passed. There was no sheltering from the cold and the frost so he gave up and crawled to where Lew was positioned overlooking the valley and the forested slope and the jagged black ridge beyond.

"About time," Lew said. His breath was white puffs of steam. "I was wondering when you'd wake up."

"I was dreaming about my mother's peach cobbler."

"How's our friend doing?"

"Still dead," Henry whispered.

Lew handed over his canteen and told him to take a drink. Henry gave it a slosh, uncapped it, and took a sip. The liquor burn went down his throat and was like a sun flaring in his belly. It was a concoction of grapefruit juice and 190 proof ethanol. He drank again and took a third drink and passed the canteen back to Lew.

"Feel them?" Lew whispered, his breath hanging in the air.

Henry could not make them out against the boulders and the brush, the snow mantling the earth, but they were there, he knew it. It was hard to look for long without blinking and blinking. Then he saw something moving through the underbrush.

"Yes," he said, and he slid the .45 from inside his parka. He touched at his pocket where his letters were collected. He let his mouth to open, to hear better.

The radio crackled and wheezed.

"You half a motherfucker," Lew hissed. He folded his body around the radio to muffle the sound and dropped to the bottom of their redoubt, scraping away a path of frost and shattering icicles that rained down on him where he collided with the dead soldier.

When Henry looked again there was a ghostly figure bent forward and crossing the traverse of their position. It was incredible to see the white silent phantom movement, dark and shadowy and obscure, the probing patrols come first to draw fire and test the strength of the front line. Then another appeared, as if conjured from the wind and the snow. Henry prodded for Lew with the toe of his boot. Another and then another appeared, the short barrels of machine guns jutting from their hips. He felt a shiver of fear sweep through him and could not breathe. He shrank as near to the rock as possible as they passed on both sides of the stony lair.

"What are the haps?" Lew whispered as he climbed back up the curved channel of stone.

Henry turned his head and put his finger to his lips, shushing him silent. The wind lifted a banner of snow, and the apparitions disappeared as suddenly as they had appeared. Then the wind dropped and they were there again, so many of them no wind could hide them.

Lew let go his hold and slid back down into the curved channel.

"They are slowly coming quick," he repeated into the radio.

Still more were coming, wave after wave, as if erected from the earth and snow, sifting through the night, wearing quilted jackets, covering ground silently, their white shapes flickering and dynamic in the swirling snow banner.

The radio crackled and Lew cursed it.

"Beaucoup Chinese," Lew hissed. "Beaucoup Chinese."

The patrols kept coming, white and shrouded and silent, and were fantastic enough to make Henry's jaw open.

"I miss you," he whispered. "I miss you so much." He ached with the pain of the thought as the shadowy figures kept coming. He began to pick up small gestures and the soft sounds they made as he watched the soldiers stream by below him. More came up, filling in behind the patrols and massing in their front, waiting for the order to commit.

He filled with fear and anguish for the men on line who would receive the brunt of this first attack. How long would it take these patrols to cross the ground between here and there? Had the word been received? Were they ready? Would their weapons fire on so cold a night as this? He could not bear how long this forever moment as he waited and waited for what he knew was coming.

"Breathe," a voice whispered close to his ear. Lew had crawled up beside him. "Breathe," he whispered again.

Then a star shell climbed slowly in the night's black atmosphere, paused in apogee, and exploded tentacles of light. They looked away from the flame so not to candle their eyes.

In the cast light the soldiers in the valley multiplied a thousand times over. They were above and below and around them in kneeling positions, ready to rise, ready to run into battle. He'd had little idea there were so many men under arms wanting to kill them.

At first was the faint sound of sporadic firing that came from the middle of the line to their rear. The enemy had arrived at isolated points. Men were shooting. Men were fighting hand to hand. Another shell split the sky, a fiery red tail sizzling behind, and when it passed overhead was a screeching in the night, but it did not explode.

Then more white-robed soldiers came over the parallel ridge and misjudging the angle of its slope, they fell and tumbled to the bottom, stacking up behind the kneeled ranks in the valley.

In the rear the lights were opening up, the rifles and machine guns. The bows of .50-caliber and .30-caliber bullets banged the air, whip-cracked it, and broke it. Grenades were exploding. The heavies opened and the violent storm of the Quad .50s.

Then all went quiet and there was a lull and all action was suspended.

Time was interminable.

Distant trumpets called out from the high ground rising to the west and buglers beyond the ridges answered and it became an arc of eerie calls and countercalls, north, west, south, and back again. The stars seemed to multiply as if gathering to witness and then came the flowing threads of tracers and tongues of flame from mortar tubes.

"Jesus Christ," Lew said as he watched them stand and hang on to each other and then rush past them and forward into battle.

Henry's legs, hands, and arms began to shake with the excess energy pulsing through his veins. His heart beat faster and then he felt the blood drain from his face and he thought he would piss himself. In short order he felt disbelief, then fear, then anger. There were so many of them, an inexhaustible supply of men in quilted jackets, quilted pants. His heart beat so fast. If he could only sit for a moment. If only he could draw a deep breath and exhale a long sigh.

He swung his rifle up and pulled it into his shoulder. He tightened the sling and wrapped it around his forearm, but before he could fire Lew had him by the back of his neck and was dragging him from the edge of the stone embrasure. That wasn't their job. They'd done their job.

Suddenly the opening went black, a white figure rising in front of them and the barrel of a machine gun was in Lew's face.

Lew made a sound, as if his last, and dropped down the curved stone channel.

Henry raised and fired the .45 in a single motion. Weight, force, percussion, and the filled space emptied. A volley ripped the air over their heads, the bullets splatting into the rock around them and behind them, shards of granite flying past their eyes.

Henry looked down to see Lew was hit and he was licking off his fingers the blood he daubed from his chest. Henry crabbed down the stone channel and fell in next to him.

Lew smiled and told him it was a tin of raspberry jam he'd crushed and not his heart was shot. He held out his dripping fingers that Henry might have a taste, but Henry declined.

"Suit yourself," he said, and took another lick for himself.

There were explosions to the left and the right. There was a sharp zip in the air and a pinging sound and then the sound of drumfire. Splinters and concussions were coming closer with each round. Mortar fire was coming into their position.

Henry climbed back to the embrasure. Across the vast white terrain he could see a thin sharp tongue of white flame, the muzzle blast of a mortar tube and then another and shells marched up the heights and along the ridge closing on their position. Geysers of frozen earth and black smoke stalked in the air and collapsed back to the ground.

"We need to quit this place," Lew said.

Then there was a horrible screaming in the air, and the earth shook with explosion as interdiction fire roared in from marine artillery miles to the east. They knew to scuttle from their stone chamber and retrace the route they followed in. They ran and flung themselves down and ran again. They crossed into the harbor of their own lines where they took up fighting positions.

When the attack came again, Henry was inside a world of consuming fire, blinding smoke, the unremitting shock waves of explosions. When they advanced they fired and ran and died, their destination deep inside the perimeter where no artillery, no mortar, no machine gun could strike them. They fired from the hip and dropped grenades in their wake and plunged on into their interior.

The men of the line fired methodically until their guns spanged empty. Then they reloaded and fired again. Rifle barrels heated and glowed red. The BARs caught fire, but there was no end to them. There were thousands upon thousands of them passing through the line without stopping, killing on their way with bullets, grenades, and bayonets. Henry fired to his front, and the dead and wounded fell at the muzzle of his rifle. His fear was hammer-striking at the walls of his heart and he was desperate to kill and not be killed. He could hear a cry pounding in his eardrums and realized it was his own screaming voice searing his throat. Then he was firing over his head and then behind him and then they came back through and did it all over again as he squeezed off round after round, the butt plate thumping his shoulder.

The sweeps of bullets scathed the frozen air. They tore frozen dirt from the earth and blasted shards of granite from the stones that slivered their way inside legs, arms, eyes. His right calf suddenly burned hot for what tore through his pant leg and into his flesh, lead or stone, he did not know.

The words kept coming, "Marine, you die. Marine, you die," as they left more death in their shredding wake.

He could not know his unhope and his desperation, could not know it and still choose to live. He shot his rifle dry, reloaded, and again the rifle spanged empty. Lew ran for ammunition while Henry piled the white-robed bodies around their new position. He wanted to rest and wondered if they wanted to rest too.

Men were screaming in rage and fear. Men were weeping

without restraint, their fierce sobs caving their chests. Somewhere someone was gibbering, his mind broken.

Someone called for the corpsman. Everyone was calling for the corpsman, but he did not come because the first call he'd answered was phony and now the corpsman was dead with his throat cut.

They came three more times that night and each time it was the same. Bugles blared and whistles shrilled. The explosions that tore through them left them dead and wounded from lead, from steel, from stone, from each other's skull and teeth and bone fragments from the air it pushed. Henry listened to the cries and groans and convulsions of the men by his side, their eyes dim, half closed, and sunk to the place inside them where a remnant of heat and life still flickered. At first he did not understand their murmurings and then he did. They were praying and they were begging. They believed in the only thing that was left to them, but there was no hymn, no anthem, no incantation, no talisman to save them, only death and its awful plenitude of horrors.

Illumination fired throughout the night.

A marine with a flamethrower walked the ridge methodically dispatching the enemy wounded. He lashed out with roaring flames thirty feet long, burning to death anyone of them that still moved and each time was the splattering noise of napalm liquid from the nozzle fire and a cloud of black smoke. He did not stop until his tanks were empty and then he unharnessed them from his back and threw them down the ridge.

Henry knew he would never get back home and was

relieved. No longer was he burdened with the prospect of survival and return. He stabbed his knife into the earth within easy reach.

"Awful sounds," Lew said, bringing up more ammunition.

The cries of the wounded faded away as one by one they froze to death or died of wounds before they could be taken off the ridge, but there was one marine who never lost consciousness and who hung on throughout the night. He was in the darkness beyond the perimeter and some said he wasn't really one of them, and long after the battle he kept calling out to them, in a young man's voice, "Here I am . . . here I am."

Chapter 20

IN THE MORNING'S HEATLESS light a dense poison fog hung in the air from so much burned powder, from starting the engines every hour, from torn bowels, from death. Henry's ears still rang from the infinite explosions, the assaults and their endless cracking frequency. He covered his ears and closed out the world to experience a moment of muffled quiet. Held inside was the ringing sound and his head ached.

The ground was strewn with bodies coated in frost and the strew of blood was everywhere. Men, weapons, boxes, shell casings, the blown, broken, burned, and used machinery of war was everywhere. The pools of blood were shockingly crimson on the white snow in the yellow light of the bluing sky. So much life he had taken to save his own.

He flattened the palm of his hand, the letter he would write. *Dearest Mother . . . Last night we were overrun . . . A lot of killing went on . . . It's bad and it will get more bad . . . In moments I think this is where I might live for the rest of my life.*

Constant was the earthshaking barrage of artillery and the scream of the Corsairs and Mustangs tearing the overhead sky. Plane after plane flew in and scraped off its napalm.

Plane after plane, denied the night battle, was desperate to get in and eagerly unleashed its rockets, bombs, and machine guns.

The Chinese were out there, but by day they could not be seen in the snow because of their white uniforms. Their battalions were holed up and in the trees, in caves and lying camouflaged out in the open. He felt the surround of them, sheltered, hovering, waiting for when another night would come and bring its darkness.

Resigned to the sounds in his mind, Henry let his hands down and joined the turbulent world with a vague sense of restoration. He let the world spin back in and fix in his chest and he lifted himself and rolled onto his back. His wound awakened and his calf began to burn. He pushed with his heels to slide himself below the ridgeline and stood.

The wounded were flowing into the aid stations. The men of the front line had all been hit at least once, and the half who were still alive and able-bodied skidded the other half, wounded and dead, off the ridges and down the back slopes and into the positions below. Roped in stretchers, they were lowered down from the slippery rocks. Men carried them in their arms and over their shoulders.

Down below men milled through the bullet-riddled warming tents, twenty at a time, desperate for their share of restorative heat before going out again. Fifteen minutes later they rotated out and hiked back to the ridges as the next twenty entered the warmth. Some men fainted as they encountered the heat after being so cold so long.

Henry turned to shout, but he was too tired. Lew saw

him and came up anyway. They watched four men scuttling through the snow, dragging at the corners of a poncho. Slung inside was a wounded marine. The bearers traversed the hill below the ridgeline to take up the downward path. Blood came from the man's face and throat and a red tide was spreading across his chest. They were moving him as rapidly as they could when one of them slipped and fell and they dumped him. He rolled the last long way and ended in a silent unmoving heap.

"Remind me not to get wounded too bad," Henry said.

Lew swore bitterly for a while and then went back to dragging bodies in white-quilted coats to fortify their position where they would freeze in place.

Then it was their turn to go down. Together they led a procession of blinded men off the ridge, stumbling along, slowly picking their way. Lew kept telling them they weren't hurt, they were okay, they just couldn't see.

"Take your time," he said. "Don't panic, descend slowly, don't give them a silhouette."

The salvageable had found a place on the damp straw of the aid station while the worst cases were settled into the corners where they might quietly finish their lives. There was an officer, dead or alive they could not tell, his belly torn open and steam rising from between his fingers where he held them entwined. In the cold air was the intense smell of his body inside. Blood clotted bandages, morphine syrettes, broken plasma bottles littered the ground. There was another man shot through both cheekbones and another the curve of his cheek and his nose shot away. There was one had a sucking chest wound, his lungs drawing air through the bullet hole. An unraveled sheath of muscle sprawled from a torn pant leg. Red-hot fragments driven deeply into a man's body and his legs were shattered. A fist-sized hole. The men did not look human after war's subtraction: no eye, no ear, no nose, no face, no arm, no leg, no gut, no bowel, no bone, no spine, no muscle, no nerve, no breath, no heart, no brain, no faith.

The padre moved among them with a vial of oil, and assuming their faith, their contrition, and their wanting absolution, he raised his hand and intoned the words By *this anointing may the Lord forgive you in whatsoever you have failed* . . .

They let down their blind men on the straw and caped their shoulders with blankets. Beside them was a man who had no eyes. Lew told them again, in a whisper, they'd be okay, they just couldn't see, they were in the vision ward.

"I can't be here," Henry said.

"Quit being a baby," Lew said, and went down on his knees to bare Henry's calf. A channel was gouged through the flesh and the underlying meat. The wound was black and crusted, cold and stiff. Lew stopped a corpsman who poked at it. The corpsman told him to bend his leg back and when he did he doused it with iodine and then attended to the more needy. His orders were to get these men patched up and back on the line.

All that morning they lugged ammunition up the ridge and helped the wounded off and went back up the ridge again. They humped units of fire, a day's worth, two day's worth, three. They made yet another trip. They collected a stockpile of ammunition, a BAR, replacement barrels for the machine guns, binoculars, a cardboard box full of big chocolate bars. The crack of gunfire exploded in the mountains and continued fiercely. The Chinese were hard to find in the snow, but then they'd see movement, a profile. Rifleman watched for puffs of breath and then shot the source of breath.

"Come on. Come on . . . There," Lew would say, holding the binoculars to his eyes, and Henry would squeeze the trigger on the BAR and kill a half mile away.

"God bless the BAR," Lew would say.

Gradually the sun began to set on the blackened napalm-swept land and the deep scars of bomb craters. It was hard to imagine a living thing could be left out there after what the airships had done, but each man alone in the gloaming knew what twilight meant. Flying through the night on the burned land would be phantoms more horrible than any mind of an imaginer could conjure.

Chapter 21

A s cold as it was, he still sweated. His arms and back
and legs and feet, they sweated for the effort of staying
warm and staying alive. He shed his shoepacs and dragged
off his socks for dry ones. He wanted to rest. He lay silently
in the gritty snow straining to stay awake, because he knew if
he fell asleep he would never wake up. He tried to remember
something of the past, anything: home, his mother, a horse,
but he could not. What he did last night would he be able to
do tonight?

He stood and stomped his feet and pounded his arms to
his chest and then he lay down on the cold ground and con-
templating the dure of this night he closed his eyes and then
Lew was nudging him in the ribs with his boot toe.

"Lay on this," he said, and dropped an armful of straw on
the ground beside him.

A flare went up and the sky went blue-white.

It was now thirty below zero and just as he stretched out
on the pile of straw, green tracers came over the crest of a
hill to the north. They bounced off the slopes and zoomed
straight up toward the stars and were followed by the yellow-
ish light of flares on the perimeter.

His turn awake. Isolated mines and trip flares started going off. Their reconnaissance had begun. Dark shadows moved as if wind materialized. Henry stretched forward and peered into the gloom, a mustache of frost growing over his lip. He wondered if only they might pause so he could see them, how fair that would be. He fixed on a shadow and grimly he squeezed the trigger of the BAR and the shadow disappeared as if made invisible by the rifle's abrupt sound thumping the air.

He had the passing thought he'd gone a little insane.

The first rounds of mortars began coming in. They spluttered in flight and then seemed to pause and then they struck. The mortars required of them a fearsome response and close-in artillery airbursts sent showers of red-hot steel spiking into the valley. Artillery slammed into the forest, dismasting trees. Flames lashed out and from their yellow flags spun swirls of shrapnel as spotters called in the mortar positions.

A man on the line staggered through the snow, his eardrums perforated, stretching his neck and clutching at his head before someone tackled him and dragged him down.

The lunging shadows multiplied. He could not believe it, but they were advancing through their own mortar fire. Searchlights banged the atmosphere, bursting star shells lit the night, tracers and flares and the world were lit with a considerable roar as if the sound of darkness fighting back.

Suddenly before him were the illuminated columns of thousands and thousands of men advancing. Bullets cracked in the air as the spinning fire sped past his ears. He could hear the cry of his own voice caught in his throat, pounding in his eardrums.

"Fire!" Gunny yelled from somewhere on the perimeter. "God dammit, fire!"

The bristling line exploded with gunfire for hundreds of yards. Hot shell casings sizzled on the frozen ground. Their fields of fire concentrated in weaving machines of lead and still they came like an inexorable tide.

I am nothing, Henry thought.

Then the flanks exploded with gunfire and grenades until there was no sound at all but the long unceasing sound of the world's endless thunder concentrated in one place.

They held the perimeter, but they could not kill them fast enough. The machine guns hammered again and again and still could not kill them fast enough. Henry took up the BAR and moved down the line to cover the machine gunner as he changed out the barrel. He fired clip after clip when suddenly the machine gunner made a rattling sound and stood and another bullet speared his chest and he fell on his back, breathing heavily.

"Don't let them get me," the machine gunner said. Henry lay across his body firing the BAR.

"It's okay now," the machine gunner said into Henry's ear, and then he died.

And then they were everywhere and there were so many they were killing each other just to kill one of them. He drew his .45 and fired point-blank into the running bodies lancing across the slope when two grenades rolled into his position and concussed him badly, his blood trickling from his nose and ears. He sank to his knees and fell forward on top of the BAR, the hot gun barrel burning into his parka and for some time he lay there as if dead and then he crawled in with the gathered dead. He slid beneath them, dragging a body on top of him.

As they stepped over him he slowed his heart and willed himself deeper into the frozen earth. Someone was gibbering the Lord's Prayer and then was bayoneted.

His only hope was to remain still, to not breathe and stay buried under the piles of bodies as he felt the earth for a clip of ammunition. He felt not fear but terror inside himself and determined he would rise up and kill again, not because they were trying to kill him but because the terror they made inside him was killing him. A hand grasped his wrist. Henry turned his head and it was Lew beside him flat on his belly. They waited but a moment before they climbed out. Henry raised the BAR to fire, but it was empty. He threw down the empty rifle and picked up a Thompson machine gun and pulled the trigger. The gun rose with fire each time and each time he pulled it back down until he emptied the clip into their backs, the bullets destroying spines, ribs and shoulder blades, macerating lungs and hearts.

Another flare arched overhead and in its flash of light, he found Gunny in the chaos. His lower extremities were missing, but like all the rest, something was driving him to survive. He'd pulled himself erect and was walking forward on his stumps, a knife clutched in his hand, but already they had left the battlefield and fled into the snow.

That was the first wave. They would come again, and like

a wounded bear, the division curled in on itself and with its paws it swiped out madly at the enemy. The division clung to their ever-shrinking perimeter. They fought with rifles and carbines, with knives, axes, shovels, rocks, their bare hands, and their teeth.

Chapter 22

THE MORNING WAS LOW and gray, but a wind had kicked up and would increase every hour whipping up the snow like flung gravel. All that morning Koreans kept coming in from the mountains, civilians. There were hundreds of them who'd been forced to work in the Monazite mines. They wanted to know which way it was to the sea. No one knew what else to do except point down the road in a southeasterly direction.

Henry hovered over the slat grill of an ambulance jeep and gasped for the odd strangeness of heat that blasted his body. He watched a lone figure ascending to the skyline on a distant ridge and standing erect.

"God damn fool," someone muttered, and then a single shot rang out and the figure crumpled and fell from sight.

"Whose was he?" someone else said, rocking from foot to foot.

"Damned if I know," the first one said.

"Sometimes you just can't take the waiting," Lew said.

However inconceivable, there was mail and he was handed a letter from his mother. He took off his glove and slit the seal with his sheath knife. She addressed him as *My Dearest Son* and confessed to missing him so very much and told him she loved him more than anyone else on earth.

They say it's going to be a bad winter and I think it will be. I remember when I was a little girl the snow always came early and it was deep and the cold was most thorough and enduring. We laid up for winter barrels of apples, huge crocks of brined pork and smaller crocks of kraut. There were smoked bacons and sausages, bins of flour and meal, preserved cherries, peaches, plums, apples, and pears. On the hoof we had beef and milk, and from milk there would be cheese and butter. In coops were chickens and eggs. For sweet there was syrup and molasses . . .

The home place had roaring fires, laden tables, games and excursions. We took evening walks through the snow. Even at so young an age I felt the mortality in that season and knew it could not go on forever . . .

But tonight the oil lamps are being lit again and I am thinking of the old soldiers drinking and remembering their horses.

The old soldiers, they killed countless men. Your grand-fathers and your uncles were not innocent. In taking you away I had hoped to save you from that. Little did I know it was not for me to decide. Little did I know the futility in our departing the home place. Little did I know that all things truly wicked start from innocence.

It is only when something starts to hurt that you under-stand it.

I have recently had a very bad diagnosis. If the doctor's
word is honest I may not be here when you return. But I
am safe. Adelita is with me.

Humble yourself, do not close the door to your heart . . .
You are the inheritor. You are held aloft by the singular
strength and the will of your grandfathers. Know that you
walk with the King for you have been to Calvary.

His mother's words struck deep at his heart. She was the
only one given to him in this life, and like his own father, he
had abandoned her. His chest washed with the ache of sadness and in his throat he felt a soundless lament. In one hand
he held the knife and in the other her letter.

"What is it this time," Lew asked, gumdrops melting in
his mouth.

"Nothing," Henry said.

"Young hearts break hard."

"It's all right."

"Nothing good ever comes in a letter," Lew said. He spit
away the gumdrop and fed a stick of gum into his mouth.

Word came to them a fire team was being gathered to go
out and bring in a distant stranded outpost. They were ordered to move east by northeast and assume a forward position overlooking the reservoir and the main supply route.

"Let's go!" said a young officer.

They loaded their backs with all the ammunition they
could carry. They shouldered their weapons. There was a
radio with good range and fresh batteries and the airships
hunting from aloft. They fell in and on command stepped off

onto unknown ground. It wasn't until noon they came to the base of a hill that was their destination marked by the spoils cuffed to the fighting holes. The holes were in a crescent-shaped arc overlooking the frozen reservoir on one side, and on the other was a valley strewn with bodies. The killed of both sides were everywhere, their bones arrayed in the midst of mangled limbs.

The young officer took out a map the wind blew away before he could read it. Lew stepped forward and yelled out.

"Anyone there?"

"Who won the World Series?" a high, thin voice returned.

"Fuck you, dimwit," Lew yelled back. "We're coming in."

He was a boy not much older than Henry and he was the lone survivor. The firing pin in his M1 had snapped and he'd lost his shoes and most of his teeth. The heavy machine gun was jammed and a bullet had pierced the water jacket and its water hung to the ground in icicles. All about the gun emplacements ammo belts were draped over boulders and brush. Blood-soaked battle dressings littered the ridge. Everywhere was the detritus of war: cartridge belts, pack straps, rifle slings, empty cartridge cases, ammo boxes, clips and the bodies of men in all poses of death.

The boy's only weapons were a knife and a pile of grenades. Why he was not insane, no one could know.

"That fighting hole smells like shit. I ain't getting in there," one of them said.

"It's a good hole," the boy said. "But you suit yourself."

"Where is everyone?" the young officer asked.

"I told them not to send no one," the boy said, and looked away to the shrouded bodies he'd dragged into long file.

"We'll tie in on the left," Lew said, spurring the young officer to command.

They set out trip flares and registered their weapons. They tried the radio, but it failed them, the freezing temperatures depleting the batteries.

The young officer sent back a runner and then another. He told them they only had to last the night and they would return in the morning.

Their work finally done, they settled in for the night. Henry tucked his feet and legs into his sleeping bag, propped himself against a boulder, and under the slow wheel of the stars he peered into the blue darkness. There was a silence and as the hours of darkness passed, his mind became susceptible to the night, alive with a presence he could not see, but was translated through the earth and into his body.

"If the bastards come tonight, that's where they will come from," Lew said with a wave of his hand.

Sleep began to descend as if a winding sheet. He felt it at the backs of his eyes and it was as if a hand was lowering his eyelids. He began to wish they would come: so he could kill them and they could kill him.

"What are you going to do after the war, Lew?"

"I think I will go to Tahiti."

"What's in Tahiti?"

"Tahitians."

He was five thousand miles from home and this night

there was a current running through him. He was not yet broken but completed and final. His mind and his being were fixed and he could not name what he felt, but he did not fear their coming again and he began to wish for the warmth of violence. He tried to remember the letter he received that morning and then he did.

Chapter 23

HENRY JERKED AWAKE. SOMEHOW he'd fallen into twitching sleep. The boy was in their midst and was talking to Lew. No one seemed to know what to do with him as he wandered about.

He was saying, "A person can bleed to death pretty quick."

Henry hawked up a gob of phlegm. He rubbed at his face and then he climbed the fire step. It was a moonlit night and with the darkness came an inexplicable warming. Someone was whistling in the dark and someone else told the whistler to shut the fuck up with his whistling.

Henry kept his eyes fixed on the strip of ground before him. As the hours passed something strange began to grow inside him. He thought of Mercy. He thought, I was wrong to run. I will never run again.

Star shells and flares hissed in the cold atmosphere and when the shells' white lights expired, the darkness came back more fiercely. The sound of weapons' fire could be heard, but it was difficult to place. Across the vast white terrain he could see a thin sharp tongue of white flame, the muzzle blast of a mortar tube and then another. The mortars were finding their range. The first rounds began coming in, the shells marching up the heights and closing in on their position.

Dearest Mother . . . Your recent letter has caused such concern and there is nothing I can do . . . I am in the hellhole of the earth and it's getting worse . . . What we do there can be no stopping . . . Not for a moment, not for a second . . . They are determined to kill us and we are determined to kill them . . . I never thought about that before . . . Once it begins it cannot be stopped . . . dearest Mother, please do not die . . .

Geysers of frozen earth and black smoke stalked in the air and collapsed back to the ground and then the shells were smashing into them, concussing their bodies. It seemed a mere rush of air, but it tore off a man's cheek and another's ear and a third was attempting to put back a dislocated thumb when his body was broken in half.

The granite that surrounded them splintered and fragmented as deadly as shrapnel.

"Time to beat feet," Lew yelled and the men on the flank bailed out of their holes and scuttled down the backside of the ridge. They fell into a deep thin gully and clung to the trembling earth, waiting for the barrage to pass above them before crawling back to the ridgeline. Henry took out one of his chocolate bars and passed it around and they ate it while they waited.

"When I was a little kid," Henry said, "I'd do anything for a chocolate bar."

"Little did you know," Lew said.

A distant explosion of guns and mortars began building into a single rumbling sound that rolled their way as the heavies in the valley responded and they knew that the dying beyond the valley had begun again.

"Jesus Christ," one of them intoned, and slid on his belly to be further underground.

"Just be happy it isn't you," the boy said.

A single bugle sounded from across the valley. Then the night filled with the sounds of bugles. They knew within minutes of the first call another attack would be on the perimeter.

"My skin will crawl for the rest of my life when I hear a bugle," one of them said.

"Pipe down."

"Why?" the one said. "They might fucking know we're here?"

They scrambled back up the ridge and took their positions. A shower of white-hot sparks rained down on them. A bullet tore through Henry's sleeve. He turned to the young officer still in the shadows and held up his arm. They exchanged a knowing look and then a black circle popped in the young officer's forehead and he was dead.

A row of shadows rose out of the darkness and then they disappeared and then they appeared again. There were hundreds of them, hunched and clad in white and running with the jut of a gun barrel at their hips. They came on as if born out of the explosions. In his mind he wrote, *When this reaches you I will be dead. A lot of us will be that way.*

"Comb it out," Lew yelled, and Henry opened fire with the

BAR held in his arms and beat off the attack. He changed out the magazine and triggered again and down the line the machine gunner triggered and sent forth the mangling fire of the flat tracking machine gun, its bloody, wearying cadence the race of their pulses, the pounding of their hearts.

Still, they came on, sifting through the night, wearing their quilted jackets and fur hats and they were shot down as fast as they came.

In Henry's fighting hole the cartridge cases were now knee deep. He climbed to a higher parapet to see the fields beyond the glacis. The sheer number of dead that lay before him was overwhelming to his mind, blood and human viscera and men dragging themselves from the field of battle.

Then they were coming again and both flanks were caving in until it was as if the men were islanded on the summit and stood back to back fighting them off the ridge.

"Fix bayonets," Lew ordered, and the men fixed their bayonets, their only chance to enter their midst and break their attack.

Henry stepped out of a mortar's explosion and heaved a bayoneted carbine through the chest of the first man he encountered. He picked up the man's Thompson, held it locked to his hip, and fired; its fire climbed into the night. The cries of the wounded faded as one by one, their guts ripped open, their limbs broken, they froze to death or died of their wounds in the low brush and on the open ground.

Near morning the boy came walking in his direction. His right arm was dangling at his side and he was saying he could not make it work. He said he believed it broken, but was not sure. Just then there was an explosion and a shard of knifing shrapnel nicked the boy's carotid artery. A hot jet of blood, and he collapsed clutching at his neck. Henry applied a compress, but the boy was bleeding out. Henry cradled him in his arms until he died.

"We cannot hold," Lew said, and somehow brought the radio to life and called for artillery.

They waited for the answer to Lew's call, but it never came.

A whistle blew. Their fire faded and ceased altogether. The attack ended and there was silence and the enemy was gone and then the sound of firing began again. The enemy had flowed past them and moved on the perimeter, cutting them off. The perimeter now was encircled and they were on its outside, a half mile beyond its laagered surround.

Chapter 24

IN THE MORNING THE radio crackled with the order to withdraw, and so they were headed back down the road they'd come up. The road would be a gauntlet of enemy soldiers. They'd have to get riflemen onto the heights to secure the ridgelines and cover the flanks. For seventy-eight miles, every hill commanding the road had to be taken.

Words crackled through the radio, *guide on the bright star,* and then the radio died.

As the darkness began to lift there came Corsairs and dive bombers firing rockets, dropping bombs, and strafing the dead. Into the valley dropped silvery canisters of napalm. Then came the flying boxcars parachuting food, ammo, and supplies, much of it going to the enemy.

The men gathered around Lew and he told them to burn everything of a personal nature: photos, cards, letters, wallets, rabbits' feet.

"Etcetera," he said.

They were to keep their weapon, ammunition, bayonet, pack, and one pair socks. All else was to be burned. Everything, and then they'd start back. All that they emptied from their pockets was thrown to the ground, doused with Sterno, and incinerated. Similar fires began lighting the hilltops and ridgelines, and in the valley stronghold huge bonfires began.

Lew took out his Hawaiian shirt and paused to consider the loss of it. He stripped off and pulled on the shirt, his upper body, naked and pink, losing heat at a furious rate.

"Sweet, Lew," one of them said, and whistled.

On Henry's cartridge belt were ten clips of M1 ammunition, a wound packet, and a bayonet. He rolled his sleeping bag into a long horseshoe, tied it off, and looped it over his shoulder. He slung his rifle, picked up a BAR, and gathered what clips he could find. He charged the .45 and sheathed his knife. He kissed the letters he carried and committed them to the fire pit.

"Quit your monkeying around," Lew was saying.

"I got the hiccups," a marine was saying.

"How the hell can you get the hiccups?"

"It's time to go," Henry said, and looked to Lew — which way?

"Thataway," Lew said, pointing to the stone spur behind them.

Henry jammed his fist into a crevice and pulled himself up the first height. The rest followed as he made his way between the rocks and climbed again until he found a little path.

"So this will be easy," Lew said, and all around them the hilltops began exploding as the howitzers fired a barrage from the south. Fifteen hundred feet below them and distant in the valley, the enemy were running into the flames of the abandoned stores to save what food and clothing they could.

Inside the burning piles explosives began to detonate.

White phosphorous burst in cottony plumes. Blown and burning remnants shot through the air; fountains of flame spurted out and pirouetted through the sky. The explosions carried all manner of waste and discard. They killed the soldiers they'd fought for days and still there were thousands more between them and the column.

Below them the long column staggered into movement, black and spectral, the long march of miniature slow-moving men, deep in the coma of war, walking back down that frozen road. Inside the column was the medical train, a hundred vehicles long. Dead men had found their place on every means of conveyance possible. They were slung across the hoods of jeeps and stockpiled in trucks. They were lashed to the gun tails. They were strapped to the gun tubes, icicles of blood hanging from their bodies.

Dearest Mother . . . We are on the run . . .

On the next crest they found a lone marine, sentry to the valley below.

"Whatta ya say, Ace?" Lew said, but the marine said nothing as he maintained his vigil.

"What about him?" Henry said.

"We're going," Lew said, as if in answer to his question.

"S'long," Henry said.

"S'long," the marine said.

At a high lookout point Henry lifted the glasses and to the east was the corrugation of rugged mountains as far as a hundred mile reach. Out there were the artillerists, their mouths gaped open to equalize the pressure in their ears, their shells timed to explode in the trees and above the ground sending splinters of wood and steel and shock waves flying through the air. Here and there were towers of risen black smoke.

A shot clipped the air and Lew fell to the snow. Tongues of flame blinked in the gray. Henry stepped forward, leaned his back against the wind, and opened fire. The others came up and began to fire also. The wind collapsed and they stumbled to keep from falling.

Lew chastised them for their lack of fire discipline, the waste of so much precious ammunition.

"I am truly shot to pieces," one of the soldiers said, and fought back a fit of despair. Bullets had broken the bones in the man's legs and another bullet had gone clear through him and out the other side.

With agitated fingers he kept trying to light the cigarette. He began to cry and asked for help and Henry lit one for him. They helped him into the rocks and handed him their grenades.

Lew sent a man ahead to recon the next saddle. Henry fished a cigarette from his pack.

The returning marine half raised an arm and a gush of blood spewed from his neck. Bullets ripped combs of snow at their ankles and they returned fire. Henry pulled himself forward and held the man's head back to open his air passage, but it was too late. He was drowning in his own blood.

"How is he?" Lew yelled.

"They got him real bad," Henry yelled back.

He'd been shot through the armpit. The bullet's violent dig had found a heart line and blood swelled from the pumping wound.

"I will die soon," the man said, his voice drowning.

"Hush," Henry said, holding him to his chest.

"I'm all fucked up inside," the man managed to say. His chest was like a bloody sponge. The ground was frozen and so the pumping blood that slugged from the severed artery pooled bright red. For all Henry had seen it was still hard to believe there was so much blood in a man.

"You got any bombs on you?" the man said, his breath rapid and shallow. Between gasps he purred in his throat.

"You won't need them," Lew said softly.

"Lew," the man said, his torment so great, and Lew knelt down and took him in his arms. Lew held his face, his gurgling mouth to his neck, a .45 between them. He held him like that and then Lew pulled the trigger.

On the next ridge there came the clatter of traversing fire. Henry ducked his head and started to run, clambering up a knob and throwing himself beneath a pointed outcrop in shallow defilade. A head came up from the lip of a trench and he fired the BAR. Two grenades went off, concussing the man next to him. In a state trancelike, he began speaking what sounded to be an incomprehensible language.

A hollow roar built from below the ridgeline, the strain of climbing engines overwhelming the shearing wind, the machine-gun fire.

"The future's coming fast," Lew said, when suddenly Corsairs and Mustangs heaved into view, contrails gyring, and they were splitting the sky. Henry lifted himself and slid over upon his back. He watched as they napalmed the gun emplacement and the enemy were incinerated, and more of them yet ran from caves and from deep furrows to warm themselves by the lighted fires. They stretched their frozen hands toward the fire and when the next plane made its passage they too were burned alive.

They kept on, crossing the hilltops, following the ridgeways that joined them. They were drifting east by northeast. The sky turned from crimson to the darkening shape of violet until a chaplet of reddish light wreathed the valley below. Henry thought, Get to the water, get to the water. He broke snow, slipping and falling and getting up. When finally they scrambled up the next steep slope, the enemy manning their positions were dead of cold, the white snow piling up on their shoulders.

He pulled himself erect and marched on. He thought to keep going. He thought, This is the last time I will exist.

"What do you think our chances are?" Lew said.

"I suppose they are impossible."

"Let's just say if we don't win, there ain't no second prize."

They could hear the bugles in the distance, their ragged blatting echoing off the slopes. By that time he held no fear for the embrace of gathering darkness in that desolate landscape, no fear of the night shapes that would rise up before his eyes. His hands were cracked open and his feet ached with chilblains. Without the cold there was nothing else.

He could not remember what happened to all of them, but one by one they were gone and it was as if they'd never really existed. And then it was only him and Lew.

Chapter 25

HIS TURN AGAIN, HENRY climbed the ridge to see what was beyond. He walked alone across the open ground and found another stony ridge and another glimpse of the road and the valley below. The last twilight was draining away this day's gray, and way down below was a vehicle, the tires slewing away, careening over the edge and men jumping off in all directions.

He waved and Lew joined him and they watched the last Sabre of the day hurtle its tank of fire-jelly into the valley. It bounced and skidded and then was blossoming with black and red and yellow oily flames.

Henry and Lew slid from the ridgeline and found a crag where they harbored for the moment's rest. Lew opened a can of peanut butter and licked out the goo with his fingers. His eyes were sunken in his face, his fingers white as paper. He was as if an old man exhausted by a long life and retired to the porch.

"What are we gonna do?" Henry said.

"They're down there and we're up here," Lew said, sucking his fingers.

"Should we help?"

"If we do, who's going to help us?"

They got up again and slogged on and then there was a ridge where could be seen the vast lake in the distance, with open spaces of black ice where the wind had blown away the snow. They watched the lake, the landscape white, gray, and black, making their decision.

As the light faded the frozen lake turned to gold. A strand of thought came into his mind and he did not recognize it as such, did not recognize it as thought or the working of his mind. He was wandering somewhere between reality and vision.

"This is some kind of bad shit," Lew was saying.

"I feel like I already died and I'm just walking with you for a while. What do you think our chances are?"

"Fifty–fifty."

"In whose favor?"

"Ours," Lew said.

In his mind Henry saw again the long wounded column bristling with weapons and armed men unwilling to die.

"Time to giddyup."

"Not yet," Henry said, pointing to the lake.

They watched in silence as the icy surface of the reservoir began to move. There were thousands of them. They'd been on the white ice the whole afternoon under white sheets and canvases, having marched ten miles down lake and now they were on their hands and knees and crawling south toward the shore's stony rim where they'd join the battle. Already their silhouettes were moving onto the ridgeline.

Henry and Lew moved out again, letting the land make

decisions for them. They picked up a frozen stream and then a winding stone trail that passed through an evergreen forest moving slowly. They went down the trail, settling on one foot, then the other, sometimes no more than twenty-five yards in three minutes. It was snowing again and there was no visibility and they could smell smoke and came to a clearing and then a shoreline where suddenly before them was the vast frozen reservoir.

"I say we head onto the ice," Lew said.

"Stay close to shore?"

"Maybe. Maybe not."

They stepped onto the frozen plane and moved ever east. Near the shoreline lunules of snow waved across the ice and farther out the ice was rough surfaced but clean of snow as the wind swept it away. They moved farther out, where the going was easier and in the moonlight they could see better the paths of icy chutes where the inflow of streams and rivers was crowned and frozen. Farther out and they were periodically hidden inside a white cloak of snow. The ice groaned and cracked. The air was metallic with cold and tasted like a mouthful of gin.

To the north they could see the wavering black silhouettes of soldiers crossing. At first there were a few and then the snow curtain opened and there were so many. They could not tell who they were and began to tack for cover along the shoreline when a machine gun opened up on them.

There came the sound of an engine in the sky and then another, the engines screaming and straining. It scraped low and its underbelly exploded the snow in the tree tops.

The first Corsair dropped its tanks and flames shot from the blackened gun ports as the napalm bounced and splattered fire. Parts began to fly from the Corsair's fuselage. It speared into a low altitude as it passed over their heads, a burning trail of streaming fuel in its wake. The air dazzled with a flaming whiteness that smudged and smoked. As the ice rushed up to meet it a wing folded and it began to roll. When the pilot ejected, his chute was no more than a rag of laundry against the moon's watery light.

"You certainly don't see that very often," Lew said.

They waited and then walked on. The snow was blowing again and they were standing inside a skim of ash and gaseous oily melt-water pooling the ice. The napalm fires roared and blazed and the smoke rolled over them leaving behind the charred bones of men.

Then there came a grumbling in the sky and the second plane suddenly materialized. Tracers poured in from gun emplacements and converged and poured onto the wings. There was a puff of blue smoke and the plane wobbled and fell out of its turn. Slowly it rolled over and went into a long glide traversing the lake and disappearing into the mountains. There was a whispering in the sky and before they could move they were engulfed in a wall of flame. There was another explosion, its forces spreading across the ice. It slapped them down and sent them spinning across the surface.

"Lew," Henry groaned.

He stood up and fell over and then he stood again.

The flaying wind bore down on him and the numbing shock of a bullet stroked his body. A spatter of bullets stripped the air. A man thirty yards away was holding the gun. Henry shook his head in disbelief and lunged forward and at the same time aimed unerringly, firing his own weapon and shot the man through his teeth.

"Go to hell," Henry screamed, and was without guilt or shame and wanted only to kill. The skin was badly bruised and broken across his shoulders, but otherwise he was still able. He sucked in his lips and hurried forward, desperate to find Lew.

Shells were bursting around him. White phosphorous broke the icy air and exploded twenty-five yards to his left in a great flash of lighting. The next one exploded to the front and then a third one to his left. They were joining, as if bolides colliding in space. The next round would find him. He jumped up and ran, the shell exploding on the very spot he'd fled. There was an overwhelming flash of light and the concussion sent him skidding across the ice.

He stood, another flash, and he was caught on the near edge of the shell's bursting radius. It threw him backward, his feet flying out from under him. The sudden change in the air pressure punched his lungs, the explosion sucking the air out of him. The shock of the explosion vibrated in his spine. He tried to catch his breath.

He felt cold and wet. He felt his eyes swelling shut.

The first sound he heard was the blood beating in his eardrums. He was on fire.

Move, he told himself, but his body would not move.

"Move," he said aloud, intent that his body obey his command and he stood up.

The hot gates opened on him again. Another inferno lashed out at him, a curving unbreaking wave of violent flame caught him against his back and swirled between his legs and embraced him and knocked him down.

He held his breath. He cried in his mind. He did not want to breathe the fire into his lungs. His vision blackened as his eyes were swelling shut. Try as he might, he could not reach to put out the flames. His back felt as if burning nails had been melted into it.

Lew fell down next to him and cut open Henry's clothes and then cut into his burning skin, his hands sizzling on the hot fragments. He stuffed handfuls of snow into the holes, and still they burned, the phosphorous taking the water from his skin down to the bone. Bullets skimmed the ice, but Lew kept cutting away and loading snow onto Henry's back.

"We need to get out of here," Lew said.

"My legs don't work too good."

"They'll work."

"I can't take anymore," Henry said, weeping.

"Come on, buddy," Lew said, and then he was dragging him by his collar across the ice.

Chapter 26

WHEN HENRY CAME TO, he was wrapped in woolen blankets and drifting across a vast plane of moonlit whiteness. The moon was so bright it stole the spangling starlight and made the heavens blue as skin. He charted its mountains and dry rivers and its deeply shadowed canyons.

Then there was sound: the muffled scree of runners sliding over ice. He was on a wooden sled and Lew was drawing him east across the frozen lake.

The pace was slow and timeless. Lew walked ahead, as effortlessly as a wolf. He did not know how far they traveled. He went in and out of sleep as he was conveyed on the ice under darkness. A troop of companionate dogs had picked them up and trotted alongside, flanking the fashioned sled.

He remembered as a little boy riding a horse-drawn sleigh into the forest to cut down the Christmas tree, the chuff of the horses' hooves, his grandfather seated beside him. The fine powdery snow found his head and face and wreathed his neck. The snow was deep and the brush outgrew the hanging trail that wrapped the mountain. The first darkness was rising from the depths of the earth. Necks arched and shoulders hunched the horses trod on through shadow and snow. How enduring and resolute they were. From the wet pines came the sharp note of turpentine. The day's golden time had passed and the full-rayed sun had become a diffusion of reds and violets. Night was coming on. Deer vanished through distant thickets to appear on a more distant ridge. They climbed higher to where the setting sun had shed a bluish twilight over the land and the cloudless sky and it was there they found their Christmas tree.

They came to the edge of the ice and a steep path leading into the craggy rocks and there came the sound of barking dogs and the dogs traveling with them sent up a howl. Lew helped him to his feet and he was suddenly cold and cried out and began to shiver. They staggered up the path and entered a cemetery and passed through its perimeter, a line of brush, and came into a small village of shuttered huts with tin roofs. Beside one hut stood an old man bundled in furs, a team of iron-shod bullocks head yoked to a sledge behind him, a goad balanced on his matted shoulder. He bowed from the waist and when he did binoculars dangled from a strap at his neck. With one hand he indicated they continue following the path; with the other hand he invited them into the hut.

The entrance was a wooden door on leather hinges. The old man swung back the door and the entrance became the black mouth of a warm tunnel. The hut's interior seemed to expand in size and depth, the nave the main house and wings to the north and south formed the transept of a cross. To the north was housed a milch cow and penned pheasants and a goat. There were crated chickens, a pig and guinea fowl tied by a leg.

The hut was built around its chimney and firepit and warmed by the animals' heat. There was the smell of boiling cabbage and stale beer, a teakettle. Layers of old newspapers insulated the walls.

Lew shouldered his rifle and stretched Henry out on a pallet by the fire. He asked if the pain had abated any.

"No," Henry said. "It still hurts fierce, but I don't care anymore."

Lew took off Henry's shoepacs and he felt his toes for the first time in days. He doubted he would ever again be warm, but already the heat was climbing into his body.

"Where are we?" Henry said.

"I don't know."

"My insides are frozen."

Henry knew he had only so much left inside him and when it was gone he did not know if there would be more. He thought how death might be the only way you left this place.

Lew worked on Henry's back, daubing at it with copper sulfate.

"I will see you in the next world," Henry said.

"Which one would that be?" Lew said, moving to the lesser burns on his shoulders.

"The one or the tuther."

"Let's just not count our chickens before they hatch."

There came the sound of a baby crying. Lew swept the room with a quick dark glance. He touched at his ears and nose as if to make sure they'd not fallen off. Then he shed his own shoepacs and dragged off his socks. Slowly the fire began to take the forward edge off the chill.

"You stay here and rest."

"Where are you going?" Henry said.

"I'll be right beside you."

From a black iron cauldron the old man ladled bowls of soup with cabbage, potatoes, barley, carrots, and marrow-bones. Lew tipped a bowl to his mouth and drank down the hot broth. With his fingers he fed the rest into his mouth and then he held Henry's head and helped him drink some of the broth.

The old man produced a carton of Lucky Strike. He tapped out smokes for each. He struck a wooden match and lit the ends. Lew sighed out with his first puff of smoke. He then scrutinized the cigarette at arm's length as if trying to understand the depth of pleasure it gave him and then took another long drag.

"What was that?" Henry said.

"It was snow coming off the roof and passing by the window."

"Are you sure?"

"You sleep now."

Henry tried to sleep and when next he awoke he thought that he might have. Lew held up a syrette and he nodded. Henry felt the pinch and his mind languished as he waited for the morphine to find its way through his blood.

When next he awoke an old woman hovered at a black kettle hung from a swing hook over the open flames, letting slices cut from a dead horse slide into the boiling water. Across the small room was the unsettling sight of Lew aiming his rifle at the floor. The old man knit and reknit his fingers, but Lew would not relent.

Then a trap door opened in the floor and one by one people crawled out the cellar's stony cavern and into the hut erected on top of it. They were people coughing and hacking, their chests caving each time. There was a woman with a whimpering baby. There was a pregnant woman in the pangs of labor who needed to be dragged onto the floor and finally a girl with ash rubbed on her face and her head wrapped in bandages. She stepped defiantly to the muzzle of the rifle. She unwrapped the bandages from her head. Her hair had been roughly shorn away.

"You will be safe in this village," she said, touching her fingers to the rifle's front sight and pushing it aside.

"How so?" Lew said, his finger inside the trigger guard.

In the air she wrote the letter *T* and then the letter *B*. They were in a colony for tuberculars. She told him they found the woman in labor lost on the ice. She told him the vibrations of the bombardment had brought on her labor.

Lew returned to his side.

"What's it about?" Henry asked.

"You get some sleep. Get that chill out of your bones and you'll feel better."

"Tell me a story."

"The only story I know is my own," Lew said.

"Tell me. It must be better than mine."

"There's nothing to it."

"Start at the beginning."

"Are you sleeping?"

"Yes," Henry said.

As he slept this time, his mind took refuge in the dream

world. When Lew tried to wake him, he fought him. He kicked out with his feet and scratched at the floor for a weapon as if his hands were claws. He was not afraid. He just did not want to leave the dream world where he and Mercy were gathered and whole. His mother was there and in the dream world they were undivided.

As he became conscious and the morphine wore off the pain became intense.

"You should make it out," Henry said.

"I know that."

"There ain't nothing to discuss."

"I aint leaving you. We'll get you fixed up and leave together."

"There's no remedy for getting killed."

"You ain't killed, not yet."

"I'd like a smoke," he said, and Lew lit for him a Lucky Strike.

"I thought Thanksgiving was real nice," Lew said.

"Me too."

"The girl was educated by American Methodist missionaries," Lew said, and then told him the old man used to cross the river into Siberia to hunt tigers. He was a schoolteacher and now he was an ice cutter.

"Those are dangerous animals."

"Not as dangerous as we are."

"I cannot endure this," Henry said.

"Yes, you can."

"Do you pray?"

"No," Lew said.

"Will you pray for me?"

"Yes."

Henry went back to sleep and when he awoke there was a woman nursing an infant in a cotton sling. He thought of Mercy. He remembered the way she walked, her weaving step. He thought of the letter he would write if he could. *To the girl I love . . . I have just awakened . . . If you only knew how long it has been since I have slept . . . You will never know what you have meant to me these many nights . . . I pray that you have moved on with your life and you are happy . . . You will always be inside my lonely heart . . .*

"It sure is quiet," Henry said.

"We've been hit pretty hard," Lew said.

"Time to get up," Henry said. He stood and dizzied before Lew could stop him. He collected himself and stretched his spine and felt the pull of his back skin. The pain was so great that tears ran down his face.

In the firelight women and children were asleep on a straw-covered platform. The old man sat cross-legged and with a knife was stripping the insulation from a coil of copper wire.

Henry caught his reflection in a broken mirror-glass and saw his head was shaved and his eyebrows were burned away. He lacked the cup of his ear to its in-curve rim and missing was a tiny chip in his front tooth and the third finger on his left hand. He tried to remember when he lost it, but he could not.

They took with them stew meat wrapped in waxed paper and a sack of hard-boiled eggs. There was candy the old man had scavenged from the ice and condensed milk and as much ammunition as they could carry.

They passed through the penned and tethered and stalled and caged animals and for the first time he could smell the ammoniacal stench of their waste, the sour of the mangers. They stepped into a pitch black ice-cold night. He looked about the lacquered world seeing nothing before him.

They followed the pathway's dip and rise and ascended to a place where broken-down tractors stood in a yard.

"It's time to turn for home," Henry said.

"Which way do you think?" Lew said.

Henry looked up to the sky. He sought the Polaris star and found it and was warmed and heartened by its constancy.

"Which one do you think is Earth?" Lew said, looking at the stars over his shoulder.

Soon the sky would gunmetal and tarnish like brass and go silver and inflame and be a coppery sky. When that happened, they'd be in the hell of it again.

Chapter 27

THEY STRUCK DOWN THE eastern shore of the reservoir past burned-out tanks and abandoned trucks waiting to be stripped and reconstituted. The husks reeked of diesel fuel and incinerated human. Inside were the melted, frozen remains of ammo, weaponry, and men. Lew crawled about on hands and knees inside a wrecked mail truck, digging through the letters and supplies while Henry turned in place to watch the road coming and going and both sides across the stony ditches.

"Let me know if you find something for me," Henry said over his shoulder. The flesh of his back felt dry as parchment and knotted and pulled with every movement he made.

"I don't get it," Lew said. "She told me she'd write every day."

"You find a Mr. Goodbar, I'll have one," Henry said.

Lew stood from the wrecked truck, a Mr. Goodbar and ammo clips in one hand, a holstered .38 in the other, and they tramped on. They followed an earthen dike bordering a cultivated field. The air grumbled and they crouched low and ran for cover, a lumber pile in a field. A blue fin could be seen running the ridgeline, scouring the canyon walls with its bawling noise, its weapons armed and hunting the land below. Henry put two cigarettes between his blistered lips and struck a match inside his cupped hand while they waited.

"We need a fire tonight," Henry said.

"I hear that."

The road before them was a column of shattered and burned vehicles, a jeep tipped over, the barrels of its Quad .50s twisted, burned out, and screwed into the ground. There was an overturned truck, its wheels in the air and naked legs extending from underneath, the boots taken.

They climbed into a culvert and found a harness of .30 caliber. In a sack were frozen cans of pork and beans, frozen hamburger patties, Tootsie Rolls. The wind blowing overhead. They busted open the cans with rifle butts and broke up the contents into small chunks and started a fire.

"It's a nice way to break up the day," Lew said, holding up a charred hamburger patty.

At twilight they moved on a small village. The sky was a muzzle of wet gray, a wind tearing at the air. A woman sat in her kitchen garden against a stonewall for the heat that seeped through its mass from a fire raging on the other side. Her face was soot streaked and she held a newborn infant coated with grease to ward off the flaying wind. Henry found a tin of raspberry jam and a can of Pabst Blue Ribbon. They killed an ox, skinned what strips of meat they could, and hung them from their web belts.

At the southern end they came upon a patrol of enemy soldiers bivouacked in a warehouse. Cooking smells were coming from a darkened interior. Pack mules stood by quietly, their coats bristled and frozen.

"Wait until they get the chicken plucked," Lew whispered.

They watched while the soldiers plucked a scrawny chicken and tipped it into a helmet full of garlic and boiling water. Night was falling quickly and the wet snow had yet to slacken.

"It's been plucked," Henry said.

"Let them boil it," Lew whispered, and they waited as the soldiers split boards and fed sticks of wood into the fire. From time to time they'd prod the chicken with a bayonet until finally one spoke and they all leaned in.

"For chrissakes, it's boiled," Henry hissed.

One man lit a cigarette. He inhaled the smoke and let it curl from his lips to inhale through his nostrils. He stood in the open doorway and lit another cigarette. He then unbuttoned his trousers and pissed in the mud.

Henry pointed to the man and drew a finger across his throat. When next the man exhaled he stepped forward and slashed with his knife, cutting open his mouth cheek to cheek. He plunged the knife into the man's neck and twisted and when the man fell he pulled free from the knife.

They stepped into the firelight where the soldiers' attended the chicken. Henry carried a BAR on his hip while Lew clutched an ax in one hand and a .38 in the other. Lew closed in on the nearest man and stove in his head.

The first round of bullets killed two and a third man Henry shot off his arm. He fired until the BAR jammed. He was knocked down and lost his grip on the weapon. He groped the floor and found a horse leg, pastern and hoof, and crawled to his feet and kept beating the last man long after he was dead. He found the BAR and cleared it.

"I have a situation here," Lew called out. He was crouched on the floor, the last man standing before him.

"Looks like he wants to call it off," Henry said.

"I'm not sure it's his call to make," Lew said.

The man's glasses were broken and taped together. He coughed, covering his mouth. He bowed his head. He lowered his eyes and received the last bullets from the BAR.

"Are you all right?" Henry said.

"Do I look all right?"

"No, I suppose you don't."

Lew unfolded to reveal the hilt of a knife protruding from his ribs. Henry took hold of the hilt and Lew groaned when the knife slid from his ribs. The wound closed, but blood continued to dribble in a slow incessant exudation, spotting the floor with terrible wafers. Henry dusted it with sulfa powder and wrapped it with the last compress they had.

The warmest place to sit while they ate the chicken was the backs of the dead. Heat rose from their padded jackets, their uniforms stuffed with crumpled pages from comic books for insulation.

"Do you think we'll win, Lew?"

Lew turned to straddle the chair he'd fashioned. He gnawed at the half-cooked chicken, thinking seriously about Henry's question. Then he switched to the handful of sour balls he'd found in a man's pocket.

"I think I need to sleep," Lew said, holding his side.

Henry fashioned a pallet on the floor and made sure Lew

was comfortable and well blanketed. He watched over him until finally he could stay awake no longer and crawled in next to him.

In the morning there was a strange zodiacal light haloing the sun. When he awoke it was to the sound of Lew's dice rattling on the beaten and frozen floor.

"Are you awake?" Lew said.

"Yes," Henry said.

"Am I going to die here?"

"You will never die."

Lew made a gesture and Henry looked to his right. In the depths of the warehouse, hanging from girders, were men of the division, backlit by the rising sun. They were mostly naked and hanging by their feet. Their arms were tied back with wire strung on their elbows. This caused their backs to arch and their bodies to hang in curved suspension. One had no head. Another, his eyes were gouged out, and he'd been bayoneted with bamboo spears.

"I can see not taking prisoners," Lew said, "but that is a special effort."

"We ought to cut them down," Henry said.

"Leave them," Lew said.

"We should at least cut them down."

After they cut down the men they rested. And then they were walking again and they could see a yellow glow clasped in the gray sky, the light sent up nightly over the distant port city to guide the way to the perimeter.

The snow had turned to rain. They walked the slick trail, their feet slipping in the rising mud. They were soaked and sweating inside their sodden parkas, but neither wanted to part with them, until finally Henry stopped and rid himself of his parka and quilted pants and dragged his poncho on over his field jacket and dungarees.

Refugees were taking to the roads, following the division to the sea. They too were guiding on the light. The warmer it got, the smell of the earth became offensive, even poisonous.

"Does it hurt?" Henry said.

"Sure it hurts."

Henry looked to the sky unusually bright.

"I have seen that before," he said, squinting into the sun, "but I cannot remember what you call it."

"The sun?"

"That's it."

Lew lay back on a rock, the sun glazing his skin. He sat up abruptly, a pain coursing his face, a hand to the place of his wound.

"I think I sat in the sun too long."

"Could be," Henry said, cupping the coal of his cigarette inside his hand.

"We'll sit here a while a bit."

"You've got to hold on."

"Don't tell me what I have to do," Lew said.

The wound had begun to run anew. Henry dusted it again and wrapped it with whatever material he had for a compress. He looked to the sky again. The sun had disappeared and the sky was cold and seemed so far away.

Chapter 28

THEY SLOGGED ON THROUGH the wet snow and fog, and when one stopped the other one punched and kicked him to stay awake and keep moving. The one would chivvy the other, keep moving, keep moving. They came off the ridges and onto the road where they traveled a little while and then moved back into the country. The narrow gravel road with its sharp twists and turns was a site of unnatural desolation.

What end of the world had they come to? What smell of burning sulfur and rubbish dumps? What load of bearing death? Henry picked up a stone and hurled it into the darkness. The earth's surface was a grave. The pain of the world condensed, the war burned into his back and knifed into Lew's side.

Lew made a sound of surprise. He was tottering on his legs. His face was dry and burned. His lips were cracked. His eyes were lively but held a strange haunted look.

"How you doin,' Lew?"

"In the pink. Fresh air. Stimulating atmosphere. What could be better?" he said dreamily.

But lips were quite blue and he seemed to be losing touch. His stare was heavy and murky and he'd stare at nothing, not speaking or answering.

They rested and then they were walking again and could see the fantastic yellow glow clasped in the pearl gray sky.

"There she is," Lew said, his spirits nearly played out. "Follow the light home."

That night began a thunderous barrage of shells and rockets being sent into the outskirts of the city. Their path was so sure and traceable, it was as if they were guyed on arcing steel cables to their exploding destinations beyond the docks and breakwater. All night long they shrieked and boomed and unleashed from the mouths of the guns with an ear-thumping crack. They entered the darkness and disappeared and ran through the black sky with a terrible willfulness.

Henry tried to close his eyes, but the light penetrated his lids, and when he covered his eyes with his fingers phantoms of light continued to strobe from his brain.

They trudged on through this ferrous rain and all that day they could hear the distant rumbling of the port city and by the next day they were well inside the raining steel net of the navy's sixteen-inch guns. As the weather warmed, the stench of rotting corpses and burning oil overtook the air.

Lew was humming, "Goodnight Irene," the sounds coming from deep in the column of his neck. The last few hours had been rough on him. He seemed ancient in how he walked bent at the waist with one hand clasped to his side and the other seeming to dangle at the end of his arm. He'd lost his gloves somewhere and hadn't seemed to notice. His face was without color and spotted white and he mentioned strange cramps in his legs. There was now a leakage and a wound puddle had begun to form in the chest of his blouse as if he'd taken into himself a little bit of each death he'd committed.

"We're getting close. How are you doing, Lew?"

"I have been better."

"You stay here," Henry said, "and I'll go up and have a look-see."

"I just need a minute to recover myself," Lew said.

Lew tried to sit down but ended up falling over for the attempt and they both laughed. Henry helped him set his back against a rock and wrap his arms around his legs.

"Turn for home," he said. "Henry, don't let them leave me here."

"No," Henry said. "I wouldn't do that."

Lew reached up with his arms and Henry went down on his knees and Lew held him.

"Jesus Christ, I'd do anything for a cigarette."

"We're out," Henry said.

"We didn't get to plan our trip very well."

"We're almost home, Lew."

"I had this dream of women and their legs were made of peppermint sticks."

Henry blew gently on Lew's face to warm it.

"You have to go," Lew said, clutching him by the wrist. "This is your last by god chance."

"There's time, Lew. We're going to make it."

Lew's grip strengthened and then released. He started

singing again, and when he did Henry left his side to scramble up the loose stones that littered the last slope. He climbed three more flights of land. He ducked his head low and ran crawling the last length across open ground to a crest.

He could see the city. He thought this journey to the sea would never end, but there it was. The barrage was constant gunfire from the battleships, cruisers, destroyers, and carriers firing ten miles inland to rain down an impenetrable curtain of steel as the last of the soldiers and refugees left. He lifted the binoculars and glimpsed a Sabre limping to the ocean. Suddenly it exploded and there was fire over the ocean. He lowered the binoculars and his eyes fixed on the horizon. From beyond its watery cutting lip, somewhere in the blue Sea of Japan, the nine sixteen-inch guns of the USS *Missouri* were relentlessly throwing shells into the perimeter destroying the shore installations.

He lifted the binoculars again. A lone jeep was racing through the backstreets, past tin-roofed warehouses and low-slung factories in the direction of the waterfront. They were burning warehouses of rations while the roads entering the city were clogged with the high-piled carts of refugee families. The arterials were shoulder to shoulder with thousands of refugees pushing toward the water. On the distant plain columns of enemy soldiers were streaming south, traveling the road, converging on the perimeter while the Corsairs still tore at them. He could hear the ragged blatting of the bugles.

Dense ice fog was rolling in. The jeep had disappeared and then was a speedboat skimming the water as it fled the shoreline. He watched as the last of the transports departed the harbor.

They were going to blow the city and then they did.

He watched the blast wave pulsing and expanding in every direction, bending the air as it came at him, and then it died a quarter mile from where he stood and was only a change in the air.

"I am not here," Henry whispered. "I am not here." He sought a small place inside himself, moving from obscurity to greater obscurity. He lifted on his toes to damp the tremblors traveling through the earth.

The city billowed with black smoke and there was a violent heave beneath his feet as if he were in an open boat on the washing sea. It channeled the earth in great snaking chains through fissures and rock seams and banged and echoed from the face of declivities. In isolated dimensions it continued to bang in the air and behind him and all around him.

When it was over, he went back down the ridge to tell Lew they'd been left behind, but he could not rouse him, could not see his breath, and when he felt his hand to his lips could not feel his breath. His raw whiskered cheeks were gray-white. Inside himself Henry felt a bottomless sense of loneliness.

"Lew," he said. "Sweet Lew."

He stood beneath the inflamed coppery sky and balanced his compass waist high in the palm of his hand, but the needle wouldn't move. He tapped the glass. The needle freed and wobbled north. He pivoted with the compass box as if suspended on an invisible binnacle and faced south-southwest. It was a 150 miles down the peninsula to the thirty-eighth parallel. In country were uncounted enemy divisions and they were driving in that same direction. He put all this down inside himself, inside a room with a door. In his mind he could see the room and he could see the door. He then closed the door and turned the lock.

He inventoried his personal weapons: an M1, a .45, a sheath knife, and spare clips of ammunition.

He cut the dog tag laced into Lew's boot. He searched the sky as if it held an answer.

He pivoted again and started back up the cold road he'd just come down. In a few hours it would be Christmas Eve.

Part III

As a man will bury his glowing brand in black ashes,
off on a lonely farmstead, no neighbors near,
to keep a spark alive — no need to kindle fire
from somewhere else.

Odyssey 5.540–43

Chapter 29

IT WAS A CLEAR, very dark spring night as the *Jean Carol* entered the mouth of the Great Kanawha and began making headway up the river. She was a dying tug, coming apart at the seams, and since departing St. Louis a one-and-a-half-inch pump had worked off the engine to keep her from sinking. In her wheelhouse, engine vibration, accompanied by unwonted rumblings from below, came up through the deck.

The air was warm and breathless as the river flowed beneath like molten silver. The captain, his face lit by the glowing compass inside the brass binnacle, was concluding another recitation, this one of fifteen names. Then he pulled at the bill of his cap and sighed, as if finally his journey were at end.

"Who are they?" Henry asked.

"Names of men."

"I thought as much."

"They are men I knew personally who died on this river." The captain was eating a bologna sandwich and used it to point the river's curve.

The captain had done the same when the boat entered

the Ohio below Cape Girardeau. At the time of entering the Ohio, the list had been much longer. Henry had only met him a few days ago when the captain took him on. He was coming across the country. It'd been the only information the two men exchanged and so it did not seem polite to inquire into the captain's private ways at the time.

"Anyone waiting on your return," the captain said.

"I ain't in no rush. How about you?"

"I don't either."

"My aunt."

"But no one by the description of sweetheart."

"No," Henry said.

"But I take it there is someone like that. It seems you are determined to get home, but then again you do not seem to be in a hurry. It leaves me to conclusions."

"No one by that description. It's been a long time."

"No plans?"

"Maybe do some fishing."

"You have unsettled business."

"I'd like to harden up. I had the grippe and I haven't felt right since."

The words lay in his mind as he spoke them. He did not know how much harder he could become. He did not know how much harder a man he could be than he was.

"You seem hardy enough," the captain said, and then he said, "Life's a hard school."

In that moment, anything could have been said between them and they both knew it. For days they'd stood watch together in the wheelhouse, with Henry assuming the responsibilities of the engineer. The engineer had injured himself while in a state of drunkenness.

"What was it like?" the captain said.

"It doesn't describe well. It was very cold. It's warmer here."

"I was in the war before this one," the captain said.

"We got carved up pretty good."

"It's okay to kill people if you don't enjoy it."

"Your heart does get hard. I would have gone anyway," Henry said. Then: "How do you stop knowing what you know?"

"By an act of your mind."

"What if that doesn't work?" Henry said.

"Maybe you find something else to know."

"Like what? God? Church?"

"I wouldn't recommend either but anything that heals."

"They don't heal."

"No. I don't believe they do," the captain said. "At least not what you have."

It was a conversation neither of them wanted or needed to have, the old man because he could not remember and the young man because he could not forget. Henry shook out a pair of cigarettes and lit them, passing one over and watching its ember cross the light of the small green-lit room as he did.

"It does make you appreciate the things you do in life."

"I don't know," Henry said. "Sometimes I think I'd have rather been there than anywhere else in the world."

They left behind the ever-burning lights of the towns and now there were only cabin lights pinpointing mountain darkness or in the hollows and beneath the trestles of the train-clattered bridges, the passages from glens into old oak. They traveled the waterway below stumped-out meadows and parallel to the wooden bridges where turbulent white water necked in rocky narrows before commingling with the water of the Kanawha.

Before them, the river was a flowing ribbon where scarves of fog were beginning to collect and it wasn't long before they entered a cold unmoving wall. The distant west had all but vanished in banks of fog and darkness. Somewhere back there were the charmed shabby cities, the cold, the sunlight, the great trees in their vast forests, the rocky mountains, the river colliding with the ocean, the ocean, Korea, Lew Devine.

"How long you say since you've been back?"

Henry looked across time, past a blur of painful memories, and back again. He shrugged.

The engine slowed and coughed and then it stopped altogether and then there was silence.

"What in hell," the captain said.

Henry opened the side door of the wheelhouse and stepped out. He closed the door and descended the ladder to the lower deck. He was met with the smell of bilge water, oil, grease, tobacco. Down below, in the engine room, the engineer was still drunk and cursing whoever it was who'd started up the engine again. The engineer had been drunk since Cincinnati, where he'd stumbled and clasped hold of an exhaust pipe and burned his hands. When he let go, he left the skin of his hands still hissing and crackling and smoking on the pipe's hot surface. The blisters covered his palms and his hands were red and swollen and seemed to pulse. He'd refused first aid and so the wounds were now black and leaking fluids.

Henry helped the engineer back to his cabin where he kept a parrot and locked him in. He then restarted the engine. When he returned to the wheelhouse the captain asked him where the engineer was and he explained.

"It's for the best," the captain said.

"He's in there with the bird."

"Sometimes I think that bird is not so good for him."

"The bird doesn't seem to mind."

"How's that tooth?"

"I don't know," Henry said. "It's back in Huntington."

"Then how's your tooth hole?"

"Aching a little."

They continued on through the envelope of fog, the running lights held in a sconce of whiteness. The searchlight was no good as its glare was returned to them in the window glass and blinded them in its hold. The vibration of the engine and the thump of the rods seemed to increase.

"This is the Christliest fog I ever seen."

"It's a bad fog," Henry said.

There was a brief slashing rain and it tore into the river water. Fingers of lightning quivered around them. They moved slowly ahead as the windows beaded and streaked with rivulets of fog. The captain asked if he had another cigarette, and Henry lit one and placed it between the captain's lips. The captain slowed even more and then they were barely moving, just holding against the current. They rolled slightly to the starboard, the stern came up and they regained even keel.

"I believe we touched something," the captain said. "You get in shallow water a boat will suck down and scrape. You better have a look see below."

Henry came back up with a jar of hot coffee wrapped in a cloth. The captain lived for the most on black coffee, countless cigarettes and tots of brandy. He uncapped the jar and handed it to the captain, who drank staring straight ahead into the nothingness that lay before them, as if the wheelhouse had become but a small world on an eternal river. He told the captain everything seemed to be okay down below.

"What's he doing down there?" the captain said.

"Chewing the rag with the bird."

"What are they talking about?"

"Children."

"I need you to go forward and listen so as I can tell where I am."

Henry went down the ladder and moved into the bow as the captain shut down the engine. A warm rain had begun to fall. However warm the night, the rain and fog cut him like a whetted knife. There was no dividing line between the air and the water, the low amorphous cloud having no definable base, but he could hear the current trickling under the gunnels as they continued forward.

The memory of Mercy descended upon him. It was as if a dream from which he could not awaken. She was with him and her skin was cool and the strength in her arms and legs held him and he could not move. Her mouth was wet and she was kissing him so hard he ached.

He knelt and wiped at his eyes. His jaw throbbed and he felt the skin on his back pinch and flexed his shoulders as if bee stung. For all that he'd endured he feared for what he might find, his face so damaged. Did she still love him and was there any love left inside him? He decided he was better off not knowing the answer.

The captain bounced echoes off the shore and then gave three quick blasts on the whistle. A great fish rose and splashed in the invisibility. Henry cocked his head and cupped a hand to his ear. He listened intently while cold water pearled on his skin and clothes and he gritted his teeth to hold off a shiver that threatened to rack his body. They passed through the roused smell of waste and discharge and then the air cleared.

"Can you hear anything," the captain yelled down.

"Nothing but a barking dog."

"You come on back."

Henry climbed to the wheelhouse and took up the jar of coffee. He held it for the chill in his hands and arms. Shaking, he lit a cigarette and pulled tight the collar of his jacket. Alternately, he blew hot air into his cupped hands and trod in place. He coughed and thought the best thing about the cold was that you felt nothing.

"You scared?" the captain said.

"Just cold. My tolerance isn't up to what it used to be."

"You know when to get scared?"

"When?"

"When you see me get scared. We're all right now."

"How do you know?"

"I know that dog."

He hadn't been scared in the least and wondered if that was a sign and how was it to be read. The past was coming and soon he would descend into its whelm.

They could see a black stream of river running below and the captain asked him to go forward again and look under the fog as it was beginning to lift. Henry moved up to the bow and went down on his knees. He tucked in his chin and clasped his hands to his chest. His hands ached in the cold dampness and he could not straighten his fingers for how many times they'd been frozen. One by one he could see lights coming on underneath the fog as if they'd once been extinguished and were now electrified. Where the shore met the river came a clear line, the black water meeting the black land, rusty coal barges bleeding into the flow and beneath him the phosphorescent bow wave.

He held a hand to the side of his face as a surge of pain traveled his jawline. It passed and he spit a mouthful of blood into the river. There was a tang in the air and his sweat cooled to his skin and his mouth became sweet and dry and tannic.

Each time he closed his eyes he saw her face.

He dragged a sleeve across his wet face, but soon enough it wetted again. The river was black and the tank lights, tiny pinholes in the darkness, seemed miles away, though he knew he could kick off his boots and swim to shore if he had to. It was that close, that deceptive on the river.

He stayed like that, ducked under the fog, and hand signaled to the starboard.

The *Jean Carol* moved ahead, turning slowly to port from propeller torque, and then the rudder took effect and she started to swing smartly into the main channel and deeper water. Henry stayed on his knees, on watch, as the fog lifted above the sight line of the wheelhouse and even then did not climb back up the ladder to the wheelhouse until the captain yelled down to him that he could see and the river was his again.

"I never had children," the captain said as Henry shucked the water from his coat.

"Me neither."

"I had reasons, though."

"What makes you think I don't?"

The captain paused, as if realizing the truth of the story he'd gotten himself into and was trying to decide whether to go on or not. Clearly, it was a story he did not like to tell.

"My first time across," the captain said.

"You don't have to tell me if you don't want to."

"It's all right. It was a long ways back ago. Though time as a healer is much overrated."

The lifting fog left a new world framed in the window glass where the shore lights cut the darkness more sharply than before and the sound returned and what had been cold became warm.

"My first time across," the captain said, "we were to put in at Shanghai and from there we moved up the river. It was a dirty river and I started seeing tiny bodies swolled up and floating in its water. The bosun told me they were little girls for the most and not so wanted as little boys in that place and how in time I would get used to it."

Henry carried such shadows in his own mind, the after-images burned deep in his retinas and Henry thought to tell him so but did not see any reason in it. He felt the gnaw of hunger and lit a cigarette. The captain apologized to him for the story he had told. Henry told him it was all right, but the captain insisted that he had taken liberties with their friendship and it was a story he shouldn't ought to have told.

"It's all right," Henry said. "No apology is necessary."

"It won't be long now," the captain said. "You can go and get your tooth hole looked at."

"The dog," Henry said.

"What about it?"

"What if the barking dog back there were sick or died?"

"We'd be in trouble, then, wouldn't we?"

Then came a fierce belt of dense rain that flattened the river, but it passed too quickly to be of concern and with its passing, the thump in the engine room seemed to diminish as if the bearing and crankshaft had scraped in on their own. The night remained bleak and leaden thereafter, but they could glimpse stars and the night continued warming and seemed less dangerous.

"He used to have children," the captain said.

"What happened?"

"They drowned. Them and his wife. She was real pretty and so were the children. Like angels, they were. It was a very sad event to have happened."

"That's got to do with the bird?"

"The bird was hers."

"She taught it to speak?"

"You wouldn't think it could be so, but it sounds just like her. It says everything she used to say and the two of them have regular conversations together."

"I don't know if I could live that way."

"You wouldn't have a choice now, would you."

"No, I don't suppose you would," Henry said.

"If you ask me my opinion," the captain said, "love is the foremost disease of the chest."

The night was now quiet. In moonlight the river shone like brass. The ceiling was still low and there was a thin horizon.

He looked back. Left behind were the deads and yet death still followed him. The thought was real and natural and unshakable as nature itself. There was nothing that mattered to him. There was nothing he needed. He would live on what remained.

As they neared the city, the mountains became backlit and then they rounded a wide bend and there was a long reach and they could see the city lights reflected in the weather. As they approached the outskirts of the city, they passed the walls of low-slung sulfurous factories, their corrugated walls bleeding long trails of rust into the ground. They passed the black hulks of boxcars on sidings and the sunken hulls of blistered scows, great mounds of slack coal leeching into the river. In pockets, the smell of the river burned their nostrils and streets could be seen and there was silent traffic stopped at the intersections. They passed under the steel stanchions of a bridge and then another, and under the second there was fire inside a square of cinder blocks. An iron tripod held a soot-streaked kettle suspended over the fire that flashed and shined with darting yellow light. Cats' eyes glinted in the weeds. Black silhouettes moved in the fire's glow, an encampment of paupers. A skiff had been pushed onto the concrete apron and descending from a girder were stringers of great gutted catfish. One of the men came down to where the scum and bubbles marked the water line and urinated.

"It won't be long," the captain said. "You'll be home soon."

"What about you?" Henry said.

"I'll deliver this old scow to salvage and then there'll be something else. There always is."

"I want to thank you for the ride."

"Anytime, son. It has been my pleasure. Without you, I will always be a little short-handed from now on."

"I feel like this is something I have to do."

"I understand," the captain said, saluting him and without pause, Henry returned the salute.

The captain took Henry's hands in his own and held them in the lap of his palms. He held them over the glowing compass. He cocked his head and stared into their hands, the workings of his mind writ on his troubled face. He was to say something, but then he changed his mind and gave back to Henry his hands. He took the wheel again and nothing more was said.

As the *Jean Carol* made her approach to the dock, Henry descended from the wheelhouse and took up the forward spring line.

The captain came in at an angle, stopped the engine, and then bore off. When close, he backed her engine and Henry put out the spring line. The captain worked her ahead until the *Jean Carol* was alongside the dock. Propeller wash drove down between her hull and the dock and pushed her away from the face.

Henry tossed off his seabag and stepped down after it. His legs went weak for the draw of the solid, unmoving concrete. The captain yelled down from the wheelhouse and Henry waved without looking back. He looked down the river, the boathouse where she might be. He looked to the sky. For the long way east the signal star had guided him home. He shouldered his seabag and passed into the streets and entered the fog-damp city.

Chapter 30

IT WAS AN OLD city and worn out and as if built for some future that came by but did not stop for long. The streets steamed ghostlike from the recent thrash of rain. They were dank streets into which the daylight could hardly penetrate.

He felt the eyes of the watchers as he passed by: waiting, isolated, suspicious.

Standing behind the old soaks and idlers were upright boys smoking cigarettes against the walls. They seemed content to smoke and age until they could ascend to the ranks of the sitters. It was a city of speculators who'd guessed the price of coal, lumber, labor, and now controlled such prices.

He passed in front of the Red Pony, a barroom decorated for Christmas the first year it opened. The red and green lights strung to the corners had burned eternally since. He stopped to calculate if he was old enough to buy a drink. He wasn't, but he went in anyway and took a place in the shadows and before long he had a whisky and a beer. He wondered who these people were. He did not know any of them. He needed to leave and find his way home. It'd only been a year, but he'd come so far already and home was just a little ways more.

A weariness descended upon him and he was suddenly very tired. It'd been a long journey. His mouth was hurting for the loss of the tooth earlier that day. It'd been bothering him since St. Louis, so the captain put in at Huntington and he'd had it extracted. He declined the tooth-dentist's offer of codeine and then accepted. On a whim he wanted to ask the dentist to please give him something for homecomings instead. But he didn't. He liked the dentist. He was elderly with an enchanted disposition and was missing an arm, so whatever he did was slow and methodical and he did not seem to lack in any way for the missing arm.

Henry felt the whisky high in his throat and then down his neck and into his stomach where it glowed like a small hot sun. As the codeine's ability to affect him wore off, the liquor took over with the taste of dull metals.

He had the bitter thought he'd find his father and tell him who he was, tell him Clemmie had died and never once had she spoken of him.

From the shadows, he listened to the squeak of the chalk and the clack of the balls. He looked at his watch. The hour was getting late. He ordered again.

The door opened and as more people came in he found himself in a pleasant state of mind. The door opened again, a party of men and women, and he thought he saw Mercy's brother with them. The man's face was round and florid and he sweated profusely. Trouble he did not need or want. There was something new and very dangerous inside him, the days of war shadowing his every thought. Watchful, he looked again and realized it wasn't Randall.

In short time he'd had too many. He felt he was returning from some outer boundary of human existence and thought he was in the hell of an eternal return and never arriving. But then again, maybe it was only the whisky.

He waved a hand to catch the bartender's eye.

"Is there a place to eat?"

"There's a late-night diner right down the street."

"What kind is it?"

"What kind? Why, how many kinds is there?"

Henry shrugged and put down his money. He guessed he really didn't know how many kinds.

Outside, a wall of silver rain was lashing the street. In a second-floor window was a woman leaning on her elbows smoking a cigarette, watching the rain. The smoke from her cigarette glossed and hovered. The woman in the window looked down at him and would not give way. When he looked again she waved and smiled and he waved back.

He walked into the diner where he sat on a stool, next to the plate-glass windows that looked onto the street. He did not know what he wanted to eat. The menu meant nothing to him. Then he decided. He wanted eggs, bacon, fried potatoes, and red-eyed gravy. He felt suddenly young and free, a man in the world. He'd not be haunted. The past was in the past. He'd have a little life, by god. By god, he would. He thought about delaying his return home and spending the night in a hotel room. He'd buy a bottle and lie in bed having a few sips and maybe read a newspaper or a book. He couldn't remember the last time he'd read a book. He couldn't remember the last time he'd slept in a bed. He wondered where he could find a book and if such a place as where you found books still existed in the city. He supposed the library would be closed.

A tiny perfectly formed man entered the diner and took a stool to the other side of him. He wore a tiny suit and tiny shoes, a felt hat, miniature jewelry: ring, cuff links, wristwatch. He was smoking a cigarette and carried an ivory-headed cane.

The waitress was tall for a woman and bold figured. She had big able hands and wide, flat hips. She wore her blond hair in a tight knot at the back of her head. About her neck and shoulders she wore a wide strawberry-colored scarf. She wore no jewelry on her hands, wrists or neck. She carried a pot of boiling water for tea.

The tiny man insisted the waitress take his order first: a plate of chicken livers.

She took his order and delivered it to the kitchen and then she came back around.

"Who's this?" the tiny man said, pointing at Henry.

"I don't know," the waitress said. "Unlike most people he doesn't talk too much."

"He's a good-looking young man," the man observed.

"He looks about used up to me," she said.

"I been eatin' dry bread, if you know what I mean," Henry said.

"What'll you have?"

"The sign says you serve breakfast all day long."

"I'll take care of you," she said with a wink.

When his chicken livers came out the tiny man lit another cigarette and smoked while he ate.

A drummer came in. He wore a checker-patterned suit and a derby hat. He carried the square case that contained his samples. The man eating chicken livers turned on him as soon as he touched the counter.

"Mister, do you want to fight?" he asked.

"What say?"

"Fight. Do you want to fight?"

"No sir," the drummer said cheerfully. "I am a man of peace."

"You are a bullshit artist."

The waitress set down a breakfast platter in front of Henry. She then leaned in and said something to the tiny man. They exchanged a look and she removed the bill from where it sat beside his plate.

"What does it matter?" the tiny man huffed. He dropped his fork and walked to the door where he waited until she came out with a brown paper sack and handed it to him.

"I apologize for the trouble," the tiny man told her.

"You're the devil," she said, and pinched his cheek and everyone laughed. He took his sack of food and left.

"Who's he?" Henry said when she returned.

"A foreman at the factory. He's a little off his rocker."

"What do they make there?"

"Farm machinery. Got any more questions?"

No — he shook his head and, overwhelmed with how hungry he was, he began forking food into his mouth on the one side where he had all of his teeth.

With chuffings and clankings a train could be heard starting to roll. More than one man took out his watch to check his pocket time against the train's time.

Henry ate wolfishly and when the food was gone he scraped at the traces of yolk still on his plate, his appetite still fresh.

"You're still hungry," the waitress said, and he nodded and after a moment's deliberation he ordered a plate of beans and frankfurters with mustard and chopped onions.

"Not salty enough?" she said when he reached for the salt. He told her he needed his salt and she smiled.

After the beans and frankfurters he ordered again until finally he was full and damping crumbs from the counter into his mouth with a finger. Before him were the remains of his most recent plate: a pork sandwich and red beans and rice and a tall glass of water with white cubes of ice floating at the top.

In the back he could hear dishes colliding in sink water. A man without any teeth sat at the other end of the counter dawdling over his pie and coffee. The man cut his food into huge sections and slowly eased them into his mouth. It was a moment in his life when he didn't have to be doing anything because he was eating and he wanted to enjoy it as long as he could.

Henry wished the woman would return.

When he looked again the toothless man, propped on his elbows, was snoozing at the counter. His head would bob and he would straighten for a spell and then slowly begin to subside again.

"I just can't get not hungry," Henry said when she retuned to clear his plate.

"Sometimes the body does that. It knows what it needs. I'll stodge up a little something more for you."

"No," he said. "Thank you."

The toothless man finished eating and stood, jingling coins in his pocket.

"You go ahead," the waitress said. "I'll get you next time." He thanked her and left out the door.

"You going to get in trouble with your boss letting food walk out the door?" Henry asked.

"I am the boss," she said.

She brought him a piece of lemon meringue pie and just so he knew she told him it was the last piece.

She then turned and busied herself wiping down counters. She paused to look into the mirror that backed the cash register. She glanced at herself and then she caught him looking at her before going into the kitchen. He'd never noticed how self-regarding women were. It was in the way they touched at their hair, the way they looked at their hands and feet, the way they moved as if they were experiencing themselves moving.

The dining room was now empty and the night grew slack. The day had turned into the next. He sat at the counter smoking and she was to the other side leaning on her elbows and staring out the windows at the rain spattered street. Neither moved and the only sound was the ticking of the clock.

Henry had drunk too much and eaten too much. He felt the waitress's eyes on him and turned to look at her. He smiled and pointed to his head, twirling his index finger.

She nodded and gave to him a solemn look, as if to say she understood.

"Take your time," she said, and busied herself.

When she came by again she'd fitted a cigarette into a holder and asked him if he had a match. Briefly there was smoke between them and then it cleared. After she exhaled she touched the bottom of her top lip with her rough pink tongue. Her eyes found his before he could look away.

"You seem to be the only one left," she said.

"I'll get out of your hair," he said.

"What happened?"

"Long story."

"Oh, go ahead. I am rich with time."

"Maybe some other time."

"Fair enough," she said. "We can have conversations about little things."

"How long have you owned this place?"

"Too long."

"Where else would you be?"

"I like the beach."

"The ocean?"

"I have never seen the ocean," she said, letting her head back and exhaling.

A patrol car drove by, its tires sawing the rain soaked street. The door swung open, but whoever it was changed his mind. She lit another cigarette and one for him.

"How'd you get that face?" she said.

"Korea."

"What war is that?" she said. "I don't think I heard of it."

"The one over in Korea. They call it the Korean War."

"What was it like?" she asked as she hovered by his place at the counter.

"Let's just say it sharpened my desire to be somewheres else." He said this and it made her smile.

"It was bad," she said.

"War is hell. The men are brave. What else is there to say?"

"Do you drink, or have you quit?"

"I have been known to take a drink or two."

She set out a bottle of Old Crow, two glasses, and a small pitcher of water.

"Drink that," she said, handing him one of the glasses she poured. "You look like you could use a friend."

He nodded. He drained the glass and licked the rim.

"I believe I will go now," he said, setting the glass down.

"Another?"

"I'll have another."

"I'm in no hurry," she said. "You're welcome to sit on that stool as long as you like."

"Your name's Viv?"

"It comes off as easy as it goes on," she said, unclipping the name pinned to her smock.

She looked at him with casual detachment. He read her to be weighing the possibilities. Then a faint smile creased her lips. He could see her hair was streaked with gray, but her face was still young and so too her hands and neck. Her cheeks had flushed from the whisky.

She clinked her glass against his and they both drank again.

"What is it you know," she said.

"Know?"

He drank what she'd poured him and he was coming into

something. He didn't know what. A sort of emotion he could feel that he'd never felt before. He knew the emotions by name; he'd just never felt them all.

"You know something," she said. "Your eyes have been all over me since you walked in here."

"No," he said after a long tired sigh.

"Don't piss on my leg and tell me it's raining."

"No," he said, his face masked by his tiredness.

"Would you like some company tonight?"

"Company?"

"All night long," she said, setting her glass down and leaning over the counter, her face close to his.

"I have gotten used to my own company," he said as if a whispered prayer. His mind went back to the cold and snow.

"Pucker up," she said, and she took his face in her hands and kissed him gently, her lips so soft. She held his face and then she let go.

"Forgetting isn't something you can do," she said. "You just have to wait."

By the time he stepped out onto the street the rain had blown itself out. The night that lay before him was so quiet he could hear the tone of his own footsteps.

People passed him in ones and twos and he said hello or good evening and they returned his salutation. He had the sense of old men and whispering women gathered in the shadows, shuffling from one room to the next. A light moving through rooms. Someone was carrying a lamp.

It would be chilly tonight. His feet burned on chilly nights, every time the temperature dropped below fifty degrees.

It's time to turn for home, he thought. He longed for a home feeling, but it was not coming. Overhead was the white light of the full moon. He wondered if he could be happy in the world with no more than these stars and this light and this deep night.

Chapter 31

WHEN HE AWOKE THAT morning he was lying under a bridge clinging to his sea bag. The sarvis and redbud were in bloom. Rivers of clouds were rising from the earth's surface and fueling the sky. A policeman was prodding him in the back with his nightstick. He sat up and began to shiver. The policeman asked if he was okay and he said he was. Someone said they'd seen a dead body down by the river and when he came down the bank and saw him he was sure that was what he'd found.

"I ain't dead yet," Henry said.

"You got a place to be?" the policeman asked. "You can't stay here."

"Give me a minute."

"What were you doing here?"

"Enjoying the night."

"Don't smart-mouth me."

Henry turned to look up at him and the policeman saw the side of his face that'd been turned away from him. He was a young policeman but still older than Henry. The policeman gave him a grim look, one that seemed to take a long time.

Then he said, "Can I give you a ride somewheres?"

Henry lifted his hand and gestured no.

He collected himself and passed through the ragged yellow light of the streets and then the light ran out in shadow and there was the light cast from grimy windows.

In the early morning he walked the mazy streets until he came to a street of white-framed bungalows, white-painted trees and rocks, boxwood hedges. The DDT truck passed by him, dispensing a cloudy mist. The mist enveloped him as the truck passed and the driver waved.

His own was a neighborhood where dogs were chained in front yards and the old ones sat on their evening porches with their chins on their chests. The young ones were bored and without prospect, and the promise of diminishing inheritance. Life was over even when they were still young. They were whittlers, tinkerers, mechanics, home brewers, and butchers. The nervous and discontent, with constant necessity for handwork.

There was a white picket fence and a wooden gate that opened onto a flagstone path to the front porch of his house. A honeysuckle vine twined the wooden fence and the shrubbery was broad leaved and green in the early light.

The house was old and ramshackle and on the edge of the city. He did not remember it this way, so distant and as if decaying. On the wide porch were wicker back rockers and a glider painted white. He stood in the bare dirt yard before he went up the stairs. There was a cat he did not know sitting on the porch. The cat yawned and stretched. The house was lit with a yellow light shining through the open transom and curtained windows. The cat watched him and rubbed its head against him when he stepped up.

There was a stir of the curtains and tin dishes rattling in a neighbor's garden. There was the whistle of a freight train carried from far up the river. The screen door to the porch creaked on its hinges. He turned the knob and let himself in. Coming from the kitchen were the smells of apples and cinnamon and he felt the hand of memory and a sense of the familiar slowly begin to emerge, the patterned linoleum floor, the pots of geraniums by the window, the pendulum clock on the wall, the painted wooden kitchen table.

"Who's there," a woman said, and she turned and looked at him as if in mystery. She'd not known he was coming. She dropped the glass she held back into the dishwater.

"Adelita," he said. "It's me. It's Henry Childs."

Henry knew that she could see how different his bearing. He was still young, no more than a boy, but now somewhere beyond old. She must've thought what have they done to this boy. I know what they have done to this boy. She stepped into him and gave to him a long wordless hug.

"Where did you come from?" she said into his chest.

"A long ways away," he said.

She started at the sound of his voice, as if a resurrection from the dead.

"It's been wet out there," he said.

"We could use a lot more of that," she said.

"Been dry?"

"Too dry."

"It's been a long time," he said. He didn't know what else to say. He felt a burning at the back of his eyes.

"You must be so worn out," Adelita said. "Have you eaten? Are you hungry?"

"I ate good last night."

"You must be starving by now."

She reached her hand to his cheek. She touched his cheek and ran her warm fingers down the side of his injured face. She took his arm in hers.

"You sit down and rest a bit," she said, "and then I will feed you."

"I'm not that hungry, but I'll have a bite."

She ushered him to a chair at the kitchen table and sat him down. The floor smelled of polish and there were flowers in vases, a woman's house. She went to the pantry and brought back potatoes she took to the kitchen sink to peel. She told him she been there almost since the time he left and she was nursing at the VA. She told him when the cancer came it was like a wildfire. She told him there was a very nice memorial service and she was buried at the home place in the family cemetery. She was beloved and had so many dear friends and was so kind to everyone. She told him she could stay as long as he needed her to.

"When you are ready," Adelita said, "we can go visit her."

He held up his hand and shadowed his face.

"Henry," she said, his name a question in the voice of a kind mother, and then she said, "I can be a good listener."

He closed his eyes and rubbed his temple. Every soldier knew that to tell was to remember and to remember was to experience and to experience was to kill and die all over again. So to tell was to risk death and to talk would be to lose Clemmie all over again.

How was he to say, something in me died over there with everyone of them killed. How was he to say, I have lost my mother.

He thought for a while about the things he did not want to think about. He tried to chase them from his mind.

Then he said, "It's not simple to forget and right now I'd like to stop remembering."

"The kingdom of men is a fragile kingdom," she said.

"The Lord is a man of war," he said.

She turned from the stove. She had a look in her eyes as if she were trying to understand the composition of his face, as if she were trying to understand him. He could feel her eyes on one cheek and then the other cheek, on his forehead and nose, his mouth and each temple and his hair and eyes. She softened and became lucid.

"May I see you," she said, and when he said nothing she rinsed her hands and took his left hand in hers and looked at the white burl of skin that covered his knuckle. She let down his hand and unbuttoned his shirt and slid it from his shoulders. She touched at his shoulders and turned him that light might shine on that side of his face and neck and ear. She stepped around him on that side and gently touched at the starburst scars where the bullet passed through his arm, the track marks left by the stitches. She turned his back to the light and he felt her fingers tracing the compass rose, the dozen knots in his back where the phosphorous burned into him. She asked if he felt the tightness in his skin that he surely must feel and he told her he did.

"It's a tearing feeling," he said. "It never goes away."

"Any more?" she asked.

He unbuckled his trousers, let his pants fall and directed her to his right leg. A spray of scars, as if a school of minnows, darted his leg.

"My feet are always cold," he said.

"You sit," she said, and helped him back into his shirt and trousers.

When she set the coffee down in front of him he drank it hot enough to scald his tongue and a slight tremor went through his head and shoulders.

She set a plate of fried eggs and ham and toast before him and took a place beside him at the table. She prayed to the angels that take pity upon the soldiers and that more angels would take pity upon them. After the blessing prayer he was hungry again and he ate what she'd set before him.

She sat beside him. She held her cheek with one hand and the wrist of that hand with the other.

"You are such a handsome boy," she said.

"This face?"

"Your face."

He made a sound, the hell you say.

"Handsome doesn't mean pretty," she said.

"I am sorry," he said, his voice cracking, "for not having written her more often. I read every letter she wrote."

"How were your travels?" she said.

"It was a pretty rough road between here and there."

"What do you remember most?"

"I guess I have a lot I remember but not much memory to hold it."

"Did you find what you were looking for?" she said.

"I have just wandered through. I just did what I did."

"Did you picture it to yourself as you found it?" Adelita said.

"I am not sure."

"She would be proud of you."

"I just wanted to last as long as I could."

"You did," she said. "You lasted."

She stood and went to him and wrapped him into her arms and it was not so much an act of affection as it was natural, as it is the way family carries each other.

"I thought I was done for," Henry said. He did not want to break the deep silence around him, but he was remembering.

She collected his plate and his fork and took them to the sink. When he spoke again she turned from the sink, her hands still in the water.

"The mind is a funny thing," he said.

"Sometimes it can't be explained and sometimes it needs to explain itself." She smiled at the notion expressed and when she did the faint crow's feet around her eyes made her look young and mischievous. "There are so many experiences we do not understand and yet somehow they are meaningful."

"I do not understand that," he said.

"It means it will get better," Adelita said.

"I don't know if I can."

"You are made of stronger stuff than that."

"There are a lot of days I'd just like to forget."

He broke off his telling. That was enough, and for now, the time in the past would remain unaccounted for. She busied herself with laundry and there were pots and pans to scrub and dishes and the floor to sweep. He sat teetering back and forth on the hind legs of his chair. Then he pushed against the table and stood.

"Don't leave yet," she said.

"I wasn't going anywhere."

She went to him with a tea bag and indicated he should open his mouth. She took his chin in her hand and gently packed the tea bag in the space where his tooth had been. She held his chin in her hand, her finger still pressed to the tea bag as the pain dulled. He looked up into her face, into her eyes, and he could see the flecks of color held within.

Chapter 32

THAT NIGHT, AFTER AUNT Adelita returned from her shift at the hospital and they ate dinner, they sat on the porch where after a while she quietly dozed.

On nights like this his mother would ask him to unbraid her hair and he would array it on her shoulders and brush it. Her hair was long and black and streaked with gray and white. She'd take up the brush and untangle it and then hand the brush back to him. He'd begin at her forehead and draw back slowly to where it was longest. It was how she taught him to do it. He'd brush gently, drawing the bristles through the length of her thick hair. It was a moment of taking care and he always felt suspended and peaceful. She'd reach up to take the hand that rested on her shoulder.

"You're always so good to me," she'd say.

"I miss you," he whispered.

The clock on the mantel struck the hour and it crossed his mind how strange he felt inside this house. Not this house but any house. This was the inside world that for so long he'd been away from.

Adelita reached over and covered his hand with her own.

"Did you say something, honey?"

"It's late," he said. "You must be tired."

Darkness and nighttime were the hours of haunt and despair for him. He could sleep or not. He could nightmare or not. He never knew how it would go.

"A little bit longer," she said.

He lit a cigarette and smoked quietly. In his mind he brushed some more until finally Clemmie thanked him and said good night and receded from his mind.

"Were you homesick?" Adelita said.

"I was," Henry said, "and then it didn't matter."

She kissed the tip of her finger and touched his nose.

"I have the darkest spells early in the morning and late at night. It's where I understand how people can kill themselves."

"That doesn't sound good," she said.

"I am afraid they will grow."

"What will you do?"

"I don't know. Try and get some rest. Try and get over it."

"Please get some sleep now," she said. "Please try."

"Was she in a lot of pain?"

"No," Adelita said, a fierceness in her voice. "You can rest assured she was in no pain. We saw to that."

"You go to sleep," he said.

"I will."

"Sleep well."

She stood and yawned and stretched her arms over her head. She let them sway in the air and then she let them down on his shoulders and gave him a kiss on the forehead.

When she went up the stairs he poured himself a drink. In the parlor the cat was playing with something it had found, maybe a mouse. Whatever it might have been it was gone. He spoke to the cat and it rolled onto its back and pawed the air. He was alone again, not yet lonely, and wanted little comfort: no bed, no cushion, no rug, no pillow to sleep on. He thought he would go for a walk or have another drink.

He poured himself another drink and went up the stairs. His upstairs room smelled of coal oil, wax, and ammonia. It was as he'd left it. There was a cross over the bed where he slept and photographs and baseball trophies on the high chest of drawers. The night was so still and the air was so dry he was cold in his shirtsleeves.

He set down his empty glass. From the window he had a view of the chemical plant. He opened the top drawer of his bureau. Resting on top of his clothes was the .45 and the knife with the white jig-boned handle. He slid the drawer shut.

He took off his boots and lay down. He lay there with his eyes open, feeling the ragged thing inside him. He counted the lost: his grandfather, his mother, Walter, the Gaylen horse, the father he never knew, Lew, and Mercy, and the boy he was. The past was vanished and where to find it? He realized that he was afraid being home for all that it meant.

He got up and carried his drink to the bathroom where he turned on the shower and sealed the bottom of the door with a towel to hold the steam. He nudged the stopper into place and sat on the floor by the claw-footed tub while the shower water filled for a bath. The pipes growled and rattled and heat began to emanate from the radiators. Outside the temperature was dropping.

He could not sleep that first night and lay awake thinking about how easy the thought of sleep was when he was
freezing to death. He woke up several times and finally went
outside and smoked a cigarette on the porch. He carried the
ashtray with him as he paced. A casque-headed dog slunk by
and paused to sniff the air in his direction. He went down the
steps, walked in its direction and it moved on.

Inside a light went on and he could hear tap water running
in the kitchen. For an instant he thought it his mother, but it
was Adelita in her nightclothes standing at the sink. He sat
down on the cold ground. He took a deep breath and began
to cry. It wasn't much but a little bit and then he stopped.

He went back to bed. The memories came at night when
he closed his eyes. As he had often dreamed of home when he
was there, he now dreamed of cold and desolation. That land
was a world away and yet it came to him nightly and only in
his dreams could he not ward off the visitations of memory
and experience. He shuddered and then shook to throw it off
as if memory were water or cold. But he could feel its grip
tighten inside his chest and across his belly. His eyes began to
burn. He slid from the bed and went down on his knees and
fought to breathe but he could not and could not speak and
could not cry because he could not breathe.

He remembered going down into a field with other men.
He sank down on his knees and talked to the man next to
him before he realized everyone was dead. The man staring
out at him was dead and his eyes still open. The dead looked
like big wax dolls laid out in the snow. Some, their arms were
frozen in position to hold a rifle that way and the rifles were

gone. One was in a kneeling position resting on his elbows and the top of his head was blown off and as his body froze his brain expanded and rose up out of his cranium. Another was as if cast in stone.

Late that night, his exhaustion became so pure and complete he wanted to stay awake a bit longer just to experience it. He closed his eyes and when he opened them again a bird had awakened and was beginning its morning song. His body ached for having slept in the soft bed. Sleep in a soft bed was so strange and foreign to him. He could see a band of light to the east. It was that close to sunrise.

He thought to get out of bed, but he didn't. He pulled the blanket tighter to his chest, his hands prayerfully grasping its edge. He rolled over and tried to sleep but only lay there in a spell of thought. He'd made it through another night and was not concerned. He knew in a few days time he would be too tired to dream and he would sleep again and then there would be the days in row when he could not sleep.

Outside his window the morning blued. He could hear a sewing machine. There was the faint sound of a pipe organ. It was Sunday. The room was hot and still. His hand began to shake. He gripped the window sash until it stopped. Who'd come last night in his sleep? It was someone: his mother, his father, Mercy?

Downstairs someone arrived, a woman named Madge, a friend of Adelita's. He could hear them talking.

"People steal," Madge was saying. "Plants. Any little thing you have that's nice."

"I hate to think you are right," Adelita said.

"Everything here?"

"I did have a little glass ashtray, out there on the porch," Adelita said. "But now I think it's gone."

"Who would have taken it?"

"Kids."

"Kids are like crows."

Then they were talking about him and suddenly he felt dead and risen. He felt the anguish of being alone and the spectre of his death. He got out of bed and padded quietly into the bathroom. In back of the house were his mother's planted apple, peach, cherry, and plum trees which ran down to the edge of the river.

He looked up and found his face in the glass above the washbasin. In the mirror he could see the eyes returned from hell, his face skin darkened to bronze, what the abrading wind and frigid cold and burning flames had done to his neck and face and back.

Half of it was a nice-enough face. Healed and returned to itself, half of his face was still nearer the boy's face than the man's. For all that he'd put that face through, for all that'd gone into the mind behind the face, it was still tolerable to look at from one side and revealed little of its recent past. He wondered how it could be, how this face could return and save itself from him who had been so careless with it?

Then he turned his head to the other side and there it was: the maimed ear, the scarred and contracted skin, the evidence of everything.

He cupped water and held it up to his face. It was hot and

steamy, and when he let his face into his cupped hands the warmth poured into his head and down his neck and into his shoulders. He did it again and again, sluicing the water over his skin. It made him strong in his heart, the simple act of washing his face. He'd been lost and now he wasn't. He would be again, but for now he wasn't.

He went down the stairs and in the pantry were pears preserved in jars. He opened one. They were sweet and the juices ran into his hand and down his wrist and this is where Adelita found him.

"You already have company this morning?" he said.

"That one," she said. "She's got a hundred and one stories."

"With that many it doesn't seem worth beginning."

"She gets to talking and day turns into night."

She gestured to the table and poured him a cup of coffee. She hovered over him for a bit, her hand on his shoulder and then went to the stove.

"What would you like for dinner?" she asked, busy with cracking eggs to scramble.

"No idea," he said, still pondering his immediate thoughts.

"Beef or chicken."

"Beef and some fried potatoes."

"A steak?"

"A steak would be good," Henry said.

"When I get back, how about if I make you lemon icebox pie?"

"That would be nice," he said, and this time he kissed her on the forehead.

The morning was cool and gave way to warm and thin afternoon light roseate on the gray streets and whatever green
was coming to the lawns.

Next door he could hear a woman chastising her cat for
not loving her enough. In front of the woman's house was
a bottle tree, the sun on the glass tinkling when the wind
blew. When he looked out the window he saw a white cat
sunning itself on a rock and it seemed familiar to him, a cat
he somehow knew.

A dog came onto the porch sniffing in the corners. Henry
knocked on the window and it looked to the sound. It barked
twice and then it slunk away. He lit a cigarette and went to
the percolator for another cup of coffee and there was a
knock at the front door. He carried his coffee and cigarette
into the foyer.

It was a young man who introduced himself as a reporter
for the newspaper and asked if he'd agree to talk. As the
young man spoke Henry squinted through the cigarette
smoke he was making.

"What do you want with me?"

"I just want to talk."

"I don't know what I have to say that'd be of any interest."

"You were quite a ball player."

"I played some."

"Will you play this summer?"

"No." Henry wished he'd never answered the door.

"What was it like?"

"I don't know what you are talking about."

"Korea."

"I don't have anything to tell about that."

"What's going to happen?"

"You'll have to ask the War Department."

"I thought you might have some idea."

"I don't know anything about it," Henry said.

"You must know something. Do you think we should drop the bomb?"

"What bomb?"

"The atom bomb."

"They aren't afraid of the atom bomb."

"What do you mean they aren't afraid of the bomb?"

"Just because we're afraid of the bomb doesn't mean they are."

When Adelita returned she'd been to the hospital pharmacy for ointment for his back, it being Sunday and everything closed. He told her of the visitor and it made her angry. When she saw Madge next she would give her a piece of her mind.

Chapter 33

THE LATE TULIPS WERE coming early that year, prodding their way to the light from their loamy beds. The rains had not been fierce, but warm, steady, and insistent, and however warmly it fell, when the sun set and darkness descended, there was the constant feeling of wet and cold.

To stay in bed was to stay in bed all day. To get out in the morning and walk was to walk all day and into darkness, lose himself and hitchhike until he found a driver who knew the location of his address and could land him nearby and with the few necessary rights and lefts that would take him to his door to sleep. Then the copper morning again and he'd sit on the porch wrapped in a blanket and smoke away the day and read a book, starting wherever he picked it up and remembering nothing at all.

When the sun held two days, he would scrape and paint sides of the ramshackle house or tear at the vines that tangled the backyard. Each day was new and unplanned and empty or filled. It didn't matter to him in the least. Each afternoon there was a little boy on the corner selling lemonade from a cold bucket wrapped in a towel.

As he walked the city streets the ambush of memory

lurked in the droning sound of every airplane and siren, a cry heard outside the window, darkness. A smell could turn the clock backward as he traveled ever deeper into the spring and the heat and warmth he was so desperate for. At any time he expected to see Mercy running errands, on her way to somewhere. It was an encounter he did not want to have.

Then it was a Saturday afternoon and Adelita was working a double shift at the hospital. He walked the streets and down to the river. There were two boys pulling themselves ashore in a little flat-bottomed boat having given up on their fishing for the day. The boat was tethered to a willow where they turned it over in the shadows. For a while they skipped stones across the water's black surface and then they began to pile the stones into cairns, as if possessed by the helpless need to build.

One of the boys lost interest and with a stick in hand was knocking the blossoms off the dandelion flowers that matted the grassy bank. There were children picking blackberries that grew on the waste ground, children that swung on old tires above the stagnant side streams backed and blunted against the flow of the river. There were cars without doors or windows and bobbing soft-drink bottles, a washing machine, and torn and flimsy cotton dresses ragged in the trees.

He kept walking. He passed a barbershop and in the window was an array of shaving mugs, and beside it was a drugstore with a soda fountain. A boy in the street let go a handful of paper scraps and he watched them blow away on a wind. Inside the barbershop the barber stood from the

barber chair where he'd been seated. There was a man reading a newspaper and leaning on a broom was an old Negro.

Henry went inside the drugstore and considered an ice-
cream sundae, but asked for a limeade with gas. Behind the
marble counter was a young kid, a white-jacketed soda jerk.
For some reason he derived a certain status from this job. He
performed as if to say, I know the effect I have upon people.
Henry quickly drank down the cold, tart concoction, and
when he stepped back onto the street his belly was so full of
gas he could not help but release a tremendous belch.

Eventually he stopped at a lunchroom where he sat at a
table by the front window. He ordered a hamburger sandwich and french-fried potatoes. Two little boys stood outside
with their hands on the glass. Then they let their mouths to
the glass and licked it. Their intention was to get a rise out of
him. He stuck his tongue out at them and they did the same
to him. An old woman pushing a well-sprung baby carriage
passed by on the sidewalk. A violent storm rolled in from
the west and people disappeared from the sidewalk, dodging
the rain, newspapers over their heads. It was a fierce storm,
moving rapidly, but in minutes it had quickly expended itself
and soon the sunlight was breaking through.

But that night, however tired, he could not sleep. All night
his legs jumped and it wasn't until morning that he slept for a
few hours. It was in those few hours he began to dream again.
He dreamed within the dream. He dreamed he was in battle
and was dreaming that he wasn't.

On Sunday Adelita pulled another shift at the VA and he
was on his own again.

He paused on the street outside a church and listened to the drone of the minister, then voices singing about being sheltered in the arms of God.

At noon he swung by the same lunchroom and found it open. He ordered the blue plate special: roast turkey, cranberry sauce, carrots, and mashed potatoes. A woman led in an old man and sat him in a chair. The man was a relation of hers, perhaps her father. The old man's eyes were clear, but he moved as if blind. Girls, stem thin, dressed for church, walked past the window, their posture erect and their eyes forward. A gaggle of boys followed shortly.

He climbed the stairs to his bedroom. Inside its raftered walls he found a quiet and steady peacefulness. He determined that it would be in this room, breathing its steam-heated air where he would learn to live again. He knew it could take months, even years, but hoped it would happen sooner rather than later. He was at the place of consciousness and memory. On this night he would not struggle against the storm inside him. He would be patient.

He entered the moment of first sleep where he remained until midnight and upon waking he sat up in the moonlit room, unsure of his surroundings at first, but then he recalled where he was.

He was still a boy when he first came here and he did not know why they were leaving. His memories of the home place and the Copperhead Road were vague but always remained fond. It was his grandfather's house and was as removed and secluded as a place could be.

He remembered crawling in bed with the Captain, all of

the grandchildren and great-grandchildren who were present and the Captain reading to them from his collected books. Henry could read but could not remember learning to read, and likewise, he could write but could not remember learning to write, and he could do numbers but could not remember ever learning such.

They played chess on a pine slab, the squares cut with a knife, the black ones inked and underneath was a tripod of twisted pine branches. There were no jobs at the home place, so there was no need for clocks. He could never remember being told to do something or not to do something. They worked for no one except themselves and nightly, the Captain would assemble the children on the highest porch, the domain of the feathered and winged tribe, and they'd sit at the railing, their feet dangling in space, and at the Captain's suggestion they'd mimic a cow, a bird, a horse, a donkey, a chicken, a goat, the whole menagerie of them going into a frenzy of cackling, crowing, shooing, braying, bellowing, and honking.

Then he would lie down to sleep, his bed in the highest room of the lofty timber frame house, a sparsely furnished room, barrackslike in its furnishings where out his window was the view of air and below the air was the unending furl of mountain into mountain. Once asleep, he'd have recurring dreams, profound and symbolic of devouring beasts, wild violent animals, creatures part human and part not, dreams of serpents and the bird of hieroglyph, dreams of being frozen with fright and only to be delivered at the last moment on the wings of a dream horse creature.

Someone was calling to him. It was Clemmie. He followed her voice through the cool, darkened hallway until he came to the door to her bedroom. She told him he could come in if he wanted to. It seemed the room had been closed forever until he entered and only now was it being opened as if a place unentombed. It was an airless shuttered room with the heavy scent of her soap and powder, but the room was empty.

He went back to his room. The moon outside his window was so bright he was able to read his hand. He fell to sleep again and passed into a second sleep and this one took him into the dead of night and through to morning when there would be eggs, hot biscuits and red-eye gravy, fried apples, honey, butter, fried steak, and coffee. Eating was what he knew how to do.

He awoke to a branch rattling at the window. A gust of wind was forcing its bending and a scatter of spring rain like shot pellets. In his sleep he must've dressed himself. He was sitting on the floor wearing his clothes and shoes and a jacket and was holding his hat in his hands. He'd seen so much. He'd seen so little, but he'd seen the all of it. He felt the silence and aloneness of what it must have been like to dress in his sleep and crouch on the floor.

"Is anyone there?" he said.

"Yes," he replied after a long silence of waiting.

He looked out the morning window and down on the street there was a young police officer with gold braid running up the sides of his crisp trousers. There were men next door. They were drinking and other men were roughhousing on the lawn. Old men in shirtsleeves and wide suspenders were enjoying cigars perched in their palsied fingers.

He did not know who they were and could not recall what day it was and he had the sense they'd been drinking all night.

Adelita came out to the street to talk to the young police officer. She was wearing her apron tied over her dress and tall rubber boots. She leaned on the mudded spade she carried. She'd been working in the garden. The young police officer was smiling and ducking his head as they spoke.

Later, when he went down the stairs, she was in the kitchen, the pan sizzling with bacon frying.

"What did he want?"

"These boys poured lighter fluid on a cat and set a match to it. He was looking for them."

He thought about Adelita, the losses she'd endured, her life as a nurse, her daily life of moderation and economy, haunting and tragic and sad and joyful. He then thought about the corpsmen carrying morphine syrettes in their cheeks so they would not freeze and plunging their hands into open wounds to find the bleeders, cutting into throats so someone could breathe. They answered the call whenever and they were stabbed and shot down and blown up just like everyone else.

The rain came again. It came against the window as if long broad brushstrokes. Adelita picked up her cup of tea and drank from it, holding the cup in both her hands.

He felt her affection and a desire to stay where he was and be taken care of by this woman who had taken care of his mother in her last days. He knew she would do it. But in his chest, there was an ache and an emptiness.

"Where do you go at night?" she said, not looking at him but out the kitchen window.

"I don't know," he said. "Nowhere. I just walk."

After breakfast they took their coffee together on the porch. She told him yesterday she threaded a needle so an old soldier could sew missing buttons on his clothes. It was something for him to do. When she went back to see how he was doing, he'd accidentally sewn his finger to the garment.

Chapter 34

H<small>E WALKED ON INTO</small> darkness, the western edge of the city. He passed down the wet alley between the cross-lit redbrick walls. Rusted downspouts leaked gray water in ever knocking drips. High overhead lighted windows threw squares of dirty yellow light into each other. He searched about in his mind for a time when he felt less singular, less alone and more at peace. He wanted nothing and had nothing the world wanted from him. Death had its chance with him and he had fared well. There was no man he could think of whom he would exchange places with, or become, or even whose small habits he would like to have.

He stopped in front of the house he'd been looking for. It was not so far from his own. On the mailbox was the name Malvina Devine, and there on the shadowed porch was a woman watering flower boxes where the rain could not do the work.

"Hello," he called to her.

"Hello to you," she said, after finding who it was called to her from the darkness.

"May I come up?"

"I got nothing for you," the woman said.

"I ain't asking you for anything."

"Then what is it you want?"

"I just want to talk."

Henry nodded in the woman's direction and she allowed him a guarded smile.

By the time Henry had ascended the rickety stairway, he saw there was a man there too and the man had turned in his direction. He was wearing trousers with the legs folded neatly, pinned, and tucked underneath him where his legs should have been. Henry stopped to light a cigarette and then crossed the porch floor to where the man and the woman were sitting. He rested a hand on the railing.

"Ain't you gonna say something?" the man said. "Most people have a little something they like to say."

"What's to say?"

"Isn't it a surprise?" The man's teeth were broken and the color of yellow and black.

"It is uncommon," Henry said.

"Imagine how I felt when I woke up. I was a touch surprised myself."

"How'd it happen?"

"It were three months back. We was upcountry salvaging equipment when a high cable broke away. It lashed out and knocked me down under it. I felled across a crop of ledge and that cable kept drawing. Did I mention that the cable were a mile long?"

"No."

"Wal, it did not take but a few hunnerd feet to saw off one leg above the knee and the other leg below the knee. But I'll tell you something about that. In its dragging, that cable heated and the hot cable cauterized the bleeders as it sawed and so whilst it took my legs, it left me my life."

"It was God who cauterized the bleeders," the woman said, point-blank as if it were an argument yet resolved.

"It were the cable," the man said, and they went on like that as Henry stared off. People he did not know had begun to appear and gather. A tall girl stood by the porch, a breast baby on her hip.

"P'raps," he said, "it was God's hand on the cable." This gave them pause to think and for a moment relieved him of their quiet bickering.

"The company said it were a freak accident, but you know something?"

"What?" Henry said.

"I have not heard of a accident that was not ever freak."

"I hear you," Henry said.

However much he did not want to be, he was drawn into the plight of the man and could not decide which act had been committed by God, the taking of his legs or the leaving him his life.

"Since then," the man said, "I been on the disability, the welfare, and the social security and have not done too badly."

"He just sits his days away in his wheelchair," the woman said, "bossing everybody around like he was president of the United States."

"That was then," the man said, meaning the day he lost his legs, "and now nothing happens."

"And he sits pretty heavy to boot," the woman said.

"When you are young you take life as it comes," the man said. "But when you get older you have lived some and you have a few expectations."

"Such as what expectations have you ever had?" the woman said.

"Such as being alive tomorrow."

Off the side of the house, a boy came out and lit a work light over a blocked-up green Chevrolet without wheels. The hood was cocked and its parts were strewn on the ground in front of it as if disgorged from its maw. It was in a hopeless condition but clear to see the boy had intentions of revitalizing it. He stood with his hands thrust into the back pockets of his overalls and his hair cut in the shape of a bowl.

Henry turned his attention to the woman.

"May we go inside?"

"You're not here to sell me something?"

"No, ma'am."

"There's a little fire inside," she said.

"It's a cold dark scene out there, buddy boy," the man said. Henry thought how he too carried a shadow in his mind, the after-images burned deep in his retinas.

The woman held the door and Henry bumped the man in his wheelchair over the threshold. Inside was warm and dry and there was light and cushioned chairs to sit in. The woman took out a pack of cigarettes and a small box of stick matches from her apron pocket. She studied his face as she lit one for herself and then passed them to the man who did not offer to pass them along. They were waiting for him to speak.

"I knew your son, ma'am. I am here to pay my condolences."

"Lew is dead?" she said. And then, "Lew is dead."

"I am sorry, ma'am. I thought you already knew. I only came to pay my respects."

"Who are you? How do you know?"

"I was with him, ma'am."

"In Korea?"

"In Korea."

"What happened to him?"

"We got hit pretty hard, ma'am."

"Why don't you just cut right through it," the man said. He tipped back his head and released a plume of smoke.

Henry cleared his throat and as he did he scraped back his chair. The woman took his wrist before he could stand and implored him to stay with a litany of apologies.

"I am sorry," she said. "I am so sorry. You've come all this way."

"I thought maybe you'd have known by now. I just wanted to tell you he was real brave."

"That's my Lew," she said, and she began to weep. Henry gently tugged his wrist, but when he did her grasp tightened as if she were afraid one of them were about fall.

"Now he belongs to the angels," she said.

"Yes, ma'am."

"They told me he was missing," she said. "That much I knew."

"He was very good company," Henry said, "in some very hard times."

"You couldn't be mistaken?"

"No, ma'am."

"He was a special boy," the woman said.

"Yes, ma'am. Your son was a man far above average."

"You're just a boy yourself. How old are you?"

"Old enough."

"If he wasn't before, he is now," the man said. His was a dust yellow face with red spots. He took up a walking cane he'd never be able to use, perching his hands on the crook.

"I will thank the Lord you have come to me," the woman said. "You were the last to ever see my son alive and now you are sitting in my home."

"He was like my brother."

"Do you not have a brother?"

"No, ma'am."

Henry paused.

"He didn't want me to leave him there, but I had to," he finally said.

"Of course you did. You couldn't very well carry him out."

In moments he felt like a bomb looking for a place to go off.

"He always had to win," she said. "He could even beat you at bingo."

"How bad were it?" the man asked.

"It were bad," Henry said.

"Your living, your wanting to live, does not make you bad," the man said, wagging a finger at him.

"I struggle with that," Henry said.

"Where are your wounds?"

"Ralph," the woman cried.

"I don't have any but a few," Henry said.

"Your guardian angel," the woman whispered. She had begun to weep.

"What happened to your face?"

"I cut myself shaving," Henry said, having had enough of the man.

"I will pray for you," the woman said.

"Yes, ma'am."

"It could have gone the other way, but it didn't," the man said. "Right now Lew could be visiting your people."

"Yes, sir. It could have."

"But it didn't," the man said, and then he said, "Did you get any medals?"

"A few," Henry said. "They were passing them out by the handfuls."

The woman's lower lip was caught between her teeth. Then she stood. It was time to leave. It was time for her to go into her bedroom alone and weep the loss of her son.

"Don't take any wooden nickels," the man said, extending his hand.

"No," Henry said, taking the man's hand. "I wouldn't think of it."

"He was a tough kid," the man said.

"He was as tough and hard as any man," Henry said.

Henry stood and straightened his body. He let himself out and paused on the porch to light a cigarette. He drew deeply and the tobacco crackled and sparks flew. He knew why Lew went back and it did not have anything to do with a persimmon yellow Jaguar automobile. If he hadn't gone back he would have died here or been killed and it wouldn't have mattered. It wouldn't have been for any reason at all.

Chapter 35

IT WAS A HOT moonless night when he arrived at the riverbank. The moon was cloaked in a passing gray scud, but by the time he was ready thin ribbons of moonlight were slipping through the tangled vines on the far bank.

There was the little boat that he knew he'd find tied there, the one he watched the boys use to let out on a rope from where it would float under the bridge. He walked along the riverbank to the path that led the way down to the river and sure enough he found the flat bottom boat.

He wet a finger and held it aloft.

"When the wind's in the east the fish bite least," he whispered, and boated his gear.

In the shallows and reed banks the croaking frogs went silent as he stepped into the boat. He untied it and with a long pole he pushed away from the bank and set out on the dark river. A powerful invisible current captured the boat and in no time laid it gently atop the pool. Its flat black surface repeated the image of the bridge and the moon and the shadows of the drooping willows.

He swung into the current at the head of the deep pool and where the current slowed he swung like a flat slow pendulum.

Down there the light and darkness commingled. Under the moonlight were the yellow fritillaries dancing the sky and there was a dog somewhere baying at the moon. The air was cool and there was a gentle floating silence as if the air and water were in agreement.

He lit a small lantern with a reflector that shined a spot of light on the backwater where he hoped the fish might congregate. He raised his arm and with the flick of his wrist he cast the line into the pool between the bridge and where the water toppled and necked and flowed in the direction of the great midwestern river.

"Not much luck," he said after a short while. Overhead was the night glow of the town. From the pilings there was a soft tearing sound and a gurgling as the water raked down their walls.

I am afraid these fish have seen all the bait there is to see, he thought.

He cast in the direction the rod pointed and his line carried beyond the pool, wrapped the near limb of a tree and entangled itself.

"Better have a drink," he said, and took up a highball glass he'd filled from a bottle. He downed the drink and then let out more of the tether that held him. He managed the boat to the edge of the low bank where he was able to stand and reach the limb and untangle the line. Then he took up the rope and pulled himself back into the shadows.

"After all that you better have another," he said, and laughed and agreed with himself.

On the next cast he took a strike and lost his bait and so

he rebaited from the can of night crawlers he'd dug from the garden and cast his line again. He set down the pole and mixed another cocktail. There was leftover chicken in a sack and bread and butter, mustard pickles, and potato chips.

He picked up the pole and reeled in the line and after losing both his bait and hook, thought it was a turtle he was feeding.

"Catch it and we'll make turtle soup," he said.

"Catch it with what?" he mumbled back as he pawed through the disarray in the tackle box.

"This," he said, and untangled a length of wire with a treble hook knotted at the end. He rigged and baited and cast again, the wire singing through the air, but without any luck.

He watched the floating cork. Something was at the bait. Then the cork went under and stayed. He pulled up hard to set the hook and began to reel in what had taken his hook. A fish raised the surface once and then let itself be hauled to the boat. Dropping to his knee he boated the fish, gave the hook a twist and set the fish to swim again. He'd not felt such pleasure since when he could not remember.

At midnight there was the banging sound of an explosion and the streetlights went off and then the rest of all lights extinguished in a checkerboard pattern and the final moment was complete and abrupt and soundless. The darkness on the water was made manifold as the only lights to be seen were from the few automobiles that traveled so late at night. He flinched and the little boat quaked.

"Steady," he said. Something was prodding again at the treble hook.

There was an automobile approaching from the city. He

watched the headlights come on and then he could hear the
engine. On the bridge, midspan, the automobile stopped and
a man got out. He lit a match in the darkness and touched
it to a cigarette. He looked to the white ropey water of the
downstream side.

Maybe we dropped the bomb, Henry thought.

A flight of birds crossed the moon. Before the moon their
black arrowed wings warped and straightened and warped
again. The red eye of the cigarette paced the bridge over
his head. He boated his fish pole, blew out the lantern, and
picked up the line that tied him to the bend in the riverbank.

The droning buzz of an airplane could be heard. It came
out of the east and swooped low and made another pass.

He began to argue with himself. He knew everything was
okay and yet his heart was beating fiercely inside his chest. It
was as if there was something he'd long dreaded was coming
to be and he'd been caught out in it when it was the last thing
he wanted to happen.

Then came places of light. The hospitals with their backup
generators lit up. Pinpoints of light were being made and had
begun to converge from the so many candles and kerosene
lanterns and automobiles carrying their electricity with them.
At the station an unscheduled train was arriving, a special.
The light was growing and it was coming to the river bridge.

He took the rope in both hands and began pulling against
the current. The little boat swung into the eddies that circled
the steep bank. It tangled in cattails and reeds, and the low-
hanging limbs of the willows threatened to scrape him from
the boat. He pulled hard, as hard as he could to get back to

the landing, the rope taut and shedding water as it twisted in his hands. He held steady in the shadowed place of reeds and cattails and bowered willows.

He sat down to catch his breath, to arrest his beating heart.

The smell of gasoline came to him and he turned and looked up in time to see the automobile parked on the bridge explode with flames that rose in the night to twice the height. The water flashed the color of pewter and his vision went red and then he saw the man was similarly lighted by the flames and when the flames exploded to three and four times his height the man toppled from the bridge. His body fell, flames ripping through space, splashing sideways into the black water below where he disappeared beneath the water's surface.

He wasn't simply and terribly dead, but was surrounded by death: the dead pool, the dead bridge, the dead city, the dead air.

Breathe, Henry told himself. Breathe.

He watched that place in the river until he could watch it no longer. He wished he had another drink, but the bottle was empty.

He did not know what to do. The automobile continued to burn, the flames sawing and quavering and their flagging smoke black and gaseous and roaring. A siren began its blare and did not relent and suddenly there was the roar of another great generator and another building burst with lights and glowed with singularity. Another generator joined and another and the buildings of government lit up and joined the lights of the hospital and the darkness was split and driven back to the ragged mountains.

In the dark morning as he walked, far from the scorched stanchions of the iron bridge beyond the bend in the river, he could still smell the burning.

He went to bed in the upstairs room under the eaves, but he could not find sleep. He could hear the wind in the trees. It was still dark and wouldn't be light for some time. He sat up and yawned and then he sat forward on the edge of the bed and let his wrists fall between his knees and his chin drop to his chest.

All that had happened was in him and surrounding him and he could no more set it aside than he could set aside his arm or leg. Maybe someday.

He could hear the train whistle and the clackety clack of its passing. In the air was the burning stench of oil and gasoline and flesh. He wanted a drink.

At what point did the man on the bridge understand that he would suffer life slowly and painfully until he died? Did his mind relieve him of his understanding for what was happening, or did his mind insist on living and divide so that one half struggled against the hopelessness and the greater half sought relief?

Henry lit a match off his front tooth, let the flame linger close enough to his face that he felt the heat. Nothing in the world had changed. The night was no tear in the fabric of life. It was not chaos. It was not anarchy. It was the exception that proved the rule. The great clock was still ticking.

He knew in the morning he would hear the milkman lugging his rack of rattling of bottles.

Chapter 36

THE NEXT NIGHT WHEN Henry left the house he was
wearing a short-sleeved shirt with a long tail he stuffed
into the back waist of his khakis. He thought how he was
learning again to like this dreary gray city. It was a sad city
in how optimistic and unaware in its dreaming.

He'd put a bottle of beer in his jacket pocket and when he
left out the gate he uncapped it and took a drink. The sky was
gray and cloudless. The rain and the wind had disappeared
and the weather was high and clear. He was neither happy
nor unhappy.

Inside the hotel he stopped at the cigar stand and bought a
cigar for after dinner. An encyclopedia salesman approached
him, but he was not interested. He found a chophouse and
after he ate he lit the cigar, throwing the match over his
shoulder and kicking it with his heel. Pigeons swarmed in
the square. They were intent and busy and then, as if of a
single mind, they broke and tore the air with their wings and
disappeared.

The western sky was heart red and the mountains smoked
with twilight fog. He plucked at the creases in his trousers

and then he sat down on a bench. Soon would come the darkness and then the far bright stars. He recalled the pork chop and the baked potato and green beans and peach cobbler with ice cream he'd just eaten. He remembered the man on the bridge and did not want to. He drew on his cigar, drew the soporific smoke into his mouth. He crossed and uncrossed his legs. It was time for a drink.

He took a stool in the shadows, his elbows on the bar. When he arrived it was still early, but now it was so late. The Red Pony was filling with a surge of people just arrived from some late-night event and becoming loud and raucous. A woman was drunkenly trying to get someone on the pay phone. She rifled the coin into the slot, dialed the numbers, and tilted her head into the receiver. She waited, but there was no answer on the other end. She eyed him, gave up on the pay phone, and receded into the noise. He ordered another beer and a whisky.

He was hearing the call of the past, but in that moment its granite weight lightened. He thought about wintering in the mountains. He'd raise a cabin and keep the fire going.

Not far away, there was a blond-haired woman in a dress, sitting with her legs crossed. She was watching him and yet he had the impression she was waiting for someone else. The thigh of her top leg was long and smooth and creased by a muscle where her skirt parted and let it to the light. She kept moving her hand along her thigh as if it was something she'd just discovered.

The bartender forwarded him a shot and indicated the woman who'd been trying to make the phone call as the one who'd purchased it for him. He relayed that he didn't have to drink alone as she'd like to meet him. He pointed her out as she was weaving through the crowd toward him. He thanked her as graciously as he dared for she was in a precarious state.

"What are you doing standing out like that?" the woman said, but he didn't reply.

She took a friendly swing at his shoulder and he caught her as she fell past. He held her upright and she tried to make language, and when she could not do that she began licking her tongue in the direction of his cheek.

"How about you and me go somewhere," she said.

"Sure, I'd love to," he said.

Then a look crossed her face that was not hard to read. He turned her away from him as she went down on her knees and vomited on the floor. The crowd at the bar erupted in cheers.

The drunk woman stirred and groaned. Several women bent down to attend her. Henry thought to leave, but he was there already and warmed inside the deep crowd at the bar. He continued down the road of drunkenness, perhaps on his way to a deep and profound sleep. He raised a finger when the bartender looked his way and slid his empty glass forward.

The streets sparkled with light. He watched a patrol car do a slow pass. He was enjoying the drink and noise and the feel of so many people tucked inside one place. He knew he was close to something. He wasn't sure what it was, but it seemed like there really were reasons for coming here.

I should leave now, he thought.

Then Mercy's brother, Randall, came out of the crowd, a

drink in his hand and an unlit cigarette dangling from his mouth. He approached the blond-haired woman and it was clear there was a kind of familiarity and even friendliness between them.

Henry watched him for how sudden his appearance and yet he did not turn away. It was only a matter of time before Randall saw him. His face, at first, was expressionless and then a look of recognition crossed his face and then it blackened. He set down his drink and took time to light the cigarette. He left the side of the blond-haired woman and came to the bar where Henry sat. Henry turned away but knew Randall was walking in on him.

Henry turned back to face him and lifted his glass to his lips. He had been changed over there and tonight it was as if a gift conferred. The violence that seemed to be always inside him was pleased by this encounter. He stood and squared to meet Randall, who was a head taller than Henry. He wore a crew cut and his shoulders and arms filled his white linen jacket. His fists were balled at his sides.

For some reason Randall held back. What did he see?

"What are you doing here?" Randall said. "You are going to get hurt."

"Please," Henry said, gesturing with his chin. "Get the fuck away from me."

Then he said again "please," and he reached up with a hand as if to ward him off.

A moment of fear and then anger crossed Randall's face. He took a drink.

"Nobody wants you here," Randall said. His intoxicated

breath was very close. It was hot and smelled the sour of liquor.

"I will do as I like," Henry said.

He thought about the question, what are you doing here? Inside, he felt something like cold, blunt iron prodding at him. He understood the violence of existence and did not want to ever go through such again, but here he was. There was never any going back. In the company of violence was his sense of belonging.

The barroom smelled of stale beer, human brine, cigarette smoke. The Christmas lights were so clear they etched the air. He looked down at his fists and they were the color of bone.

But Randall would not relent. He moved in closer and crowded Henry where he stood.

"Come on, then," Henry whispered. "If you have to, come on."

Randall's face darkened and his eyes were filled with anger and then he lashed out with a fist, and though Henry saw it coming, he did not block the punch. He hit Henry over the right cheek. Henry fell back against the bar. His eye was stung and clouded and black pennons radiated in his vision.

Henry squared up and measured him, and when Randall stepped in closer he let himself be hit again. Randall shot out with a right to his stomach and Henry doubled over with an anguished and involuntary sound. He caught himself before he fell and held himself as he gasped for air.

"Is that what you want?" Henry said, and Randall hit him again. Henry's lip was opened and then his nose was bleeding. He let himself be hit again and his right eye began to close.

"Is that what you want?" Henry said again, spitting his blood onto the barroom floor.

When next he lunged, Henry went down on his left hip and he drove his right boot into Randall's groin twice. Randall folded and twisted and Henry punched him in his throat and he collapsed clutching at his neck, writhing on the wet floor and desperate to breathe. His eyes and tongue bulged out and he breathed as if his last. Henry went down on top of him and struck him again and broke his nose across his face. Blood was everywhere. He would have fought him to death, but the crowd, having had their tremors of excitement, tore them apart. Henry stood over the man, his eyes bleared with pain and cursed him and spit blood on his white linen jacket.

"I'll kill you," he said. "I'll kill you dead, you son of a bitch."

Men hustled him out the door and once on the sidewalk held him against the brick wall. Henry was panting and snapping his hands in the air and then calming. He stood upright and told them it was okay and to let him be.

His mind traveled the distance from the eruption of violence to this sidewalk where he stood.

"I will be fine," he said quietly.

From the Red Pony he walked along the dense black river. It had turned a beautiful night with a splendid emerging moon, distant yellow lights contained in palls of darkness. There were the light towers of the chemical plants and into the very depths of those yellow lights, there was fog and smoke up against blackness and it was so very beautiful to him and he no longer felt purged and winnowed, but like a sinner. It was the war had taught him to call up the devil and he could feel the devil in his legs and arms.

He walked until he paused on the banks of the river.

He thought of how as a little boy he'd walk down here with his mother following the terraced stonework that led to nowhere. They'd pass beneath the willows through reticulated shade, through the reeds and the grasses to the banks of the swirling opaline water so that she could throw into the water a sealed medicine bottle with a folded note, intended for whom he did not know and did not ask. His mother had always performed such acts. She entertained superstitions derived from belief in a world without accident or mistake, where the workings were the way fate supposed them to be. For her, there was wonder to be found in a thunderstorm, a strange sound, a coincidence of numbers. For her life was desire, belief, death, and sweet despair.

The main channel was a jewel in the moonlight, refracted light beneath its inky surface. On the opposite bank, above the city, there were lights and below the lights the darkened boathouses built overtop the water's flow. The water played tricks with noises in the night making it impossible to judge their origin or distance.

He'd wanted no summoning of the past, but that's just what he'd gone and done. Upriver he fixed on the skewed window light of a single boathouse. He calculated the distance and then turned for home, his mind a torment of pain and his eyes beginning to close. He stumbled on, trying to keep a straight line. He had to clear his head. An automobile slowed behind him and a blue light strobed once. When he turned to face the light a patrol pulled alongside.

"Get in," the policeman said.

It was the young policeman he'd seen Adelita talking to, the one who was a new father. He was sucking on a Life Saver, clicking it against his teeth.

Henry let slide a stream of blood from his mouth and got into the patrol car.

"Jesus Christ," the policeman said. "How are you even walking?"

"I have some experience," he said.

"Do you know who his father is?"

"What's it matter? Behind every bastard is another one."

"I'm taking you to the hospital."

"Just take me home," Henry said.

When he arrived home he went to the backyard where he stripped to the waist and washed with the water from the hose. The water was cold on his skin and hard and his blood ran red down his body and then pink and then the water ran clear and silver.

Under this cold moonlight he felt the shimmer of self. He felt no guilt, no pain, no remorse for what he'd done. He could have killed if he wanted to, but he did not. He felt as if he understood men, their discontent, their need to see what they'd not seen before, their need to be where they'd never been. He was one of them. He'd lived in a world of killing and blood and this world was returned to him. He'd lived in the silence and ineluctable mystery of violence. He knew the hold war had on him, the gore that would never come off in this world. He knew he could have killed Mercy's brother with his hands and it was this knowledge that gave him peace.

Chapter 37

A T THE MIRROR OVER the bathroom sink Henry stitched his torn lip and split eyebrow with needle and thread. Stitch by stitch he worked the needle into his pinched skin and slowly drew out the thread until his skin was closed and the thread knotted.

In the mirror he saw Adelita appearing in the doorway behind him. She held her arms in fold and her shoulders pressed to the doorjamb.

"Can I look at you?" she said.

"I got in a fight," he said, turning to her.

She went to him and she was so close he could smell her skin. She took his face in her hands and gently turned it to one side and then the other. Her eyes were blue and clear and her gaze sustained.

"Come closer," she said, and upon further inspection she told him he'd done an adequate job and with the scissors she snipped tight the thread ends where they sprang from knots.

"You almost killed him," she said.

"Next time I will," Henry said, but he knew she did not

believe him. She did not understand he would have killed him tonight if that was his intention, but it wasn't.

"Perhaps a better use of your time is called for," she said quietly.

How could he express to her the freedom he felt this night? He was possessed by no idea other than this one. How could he tell her he had a world of his own and one that could not be conceived by her?

"Take them off and I'll wash them for you," she said, tugging at his bloody khakis.

She bent to turn on the taps and draw him a hot bath. He waited for her to leave the room that he might take off his trousers, but she didn't. She told him he didn't have anything she hadn't seen before and to hurry up before she lost her patience and inclination. He unbuckled his trousers and let them fall and tried to step out of them but tripped and slumped against her. She braced against him and held him up and he felt her strong smooth hands on his body as she helped him into the bath.

"Henry?" she said, his name an invitation to explain his mind.

He shrugged and turned his head away. He did not care to say anything. He did not want her to know what he had been through. He did not want to explain how different and how separate he was.

"What is it?" she said.

"What difference does it make?" he said. The powerful illusion of naming things held little sway with him. To say, to name this feeling, to name these thoughts, what would it matter?

"What is it?" Adelita said again, her hand tight on his shoulder, the lines in her face drawn, her voice insistent.

"I am a murderer," Henry said, his voice flat and unaffected by the words he declared.

"No," she said. "You were a soldier."

"We killed them," he said. "For what they did we killed them and we nailed their hearts to the door."

He remembered for her that morning in the warehouse. Each of their hearts was tough with muscle and in the odd light were garnet red and sketched with white and blue. He sliced open their chests and the cold blood washed through his hands, jelled and viscose, and the hearts, still dripping, he set aside while Lew watched and then he nailed them to the door of the warehouse.

"You hush yourself," she said.

"You ask me these things," he said.

"You hush," she said. "I am not afraid of you. Even if you did what you say, I still love you."

HE WAS ALONE in the front room watching the fire when Adelita came to him again. She placed a cup of tea beside him. She handed him pills and told him to take them lest his pain become a torment.

"I am all right," he said.

"Maybe you are now, but you won't be," she said, and shook them in her hand.

After he downed the pills she sat beside him and they were both quiet for a long time.

There was a rattling of the windowpane, as if someone was knocking at the door. He listened to the cat lapping its milk. He was cold and shivering and she found a sweater for him and he pulled it onto his shoulders and buttoned it.

"Snow is falling," she said.

He went to the window and the hemlocks beyond the porch were bent by the weight of the snow. One released and sprang up. A cascade of white sifted through the branches releasing more branches as it tumbled and the branches scraped the window. The tree seemed to shake the way a horse or a man might.

Headlights opened on the street and a black Oldsmobile drove past the front gate. Henry stood at the window and watched as it came by again. This time it stopped and idled at the gate.

"Don't go out there," she said. She was standing by his side.

"He won't bully me," he said. The violence was in him again, in his hands and in his mind and in his gut. It came with him. He'd brought it home with him.

"The Lord's hand will come and he will point to the way."

"I do not care to take directions from him."

"Don't make me beg," Adelita whispered, taking his arm in both of hers.

"They'll not leave me alone."

"You have your whole life ahead of you."

"What life?" Henry said.

"What do you want?"

"I don't know."

"It's finished. Can't you start over?"

"I can't imagine it," he said.

"No, not yet you can't, but you will."

He let his eyes to the darkness and felt a sense of grief and desire. He held no opinion what should happen next. He remained at the window while the black Oldsmobile sat idling in the cold. Then it drove away.

Adelita asked that he sit and drink his tea. She had something for him and she would get it. When she returned she carried an envelope. She had been waiting for a good time to give it to him and she supposed tonight was as good a time as any.

Inside was a letter from his mother.

Dear Son,

I have come from sleep this night to write to you. I am so tired and the time I have left is short. I will not be cut on having so often witnessed the no good that comes of it. My only sadness is that I will not see you again until we meet in heaven, but I am braced for what I will do.

I am moved to finally tell you about your origins. You should know of your paternity, it being the right of every human being to possess such knowledge.

There was a man, a surveyor for a coal company who came on to our land. My father, your grandfather, was away so I went with him to point out our border across the valley. This land was granted to your great-great-grandfather for his service in war and has since been

returned to the government and the money barons, the
land taxes having never been paid.

I did not know what I wanted, but he knew what he
wanted. I will not say I was against it. Afterward he said
he was sorry for what he did to me and I think he meant
it. I pulled myself together and I went home. I did not say
anything that happened, but my father, having returned,
took one look at me and picked up his rifle-gun and out he
went the way I came running from.

I will never forget the echoing report of that rifle. I have
heard it in my mind every day of my life ever since. That
man was never heard from or seen again. They came
around looking for him, but nobody ever said a word.
That day in the forest was how you came to be. My father,
your grandfather, he killed the man and I do not know
how to explain it, but that day something was killed inside
me as well . . .

I pray you are reading this for that means you have
returned to us. Be a good boy for Adelita. Love her dearly.
She has been a strong and consoling presence, a balm to
my existence.

Henry refolded the letter and placed it back in the envelope. It was strange what little effect this news had upon
him.

"My father," he said. He handed the letter to Adelita and
invited her to read it if she wished. He wanted to feel something, but inside him was as if an open mouth, empty and
silent. After all this time, there was so little he cared about.
He thought, I am my own father. I am my own.

"I apologize for how I have been," he said, lifting his eyes to Adelita.

"No," she said. "It isn't like that. We are family."

"You were so good to my mother and you have been so good to me."

"Henry Childs," she began, but then she stopped and she said, "I am the fortunate one. I lost my husband and my boys, and your mother, but not you. You came home."

It was then he told her he would be leaving soon. His time was near up and he was obligated to return.

"You don't have to go."

"It is something I have to do."

"You have put your mind to it?"

"Yes."

"When?"

"In a few days' time. It has nothing to do with this. It's been that way all along. I just did not know how to tell you."

That night he could hear her down the hall weeping. He was so tired and his body, his face hurt so much, but he waited until she found sleep before he allowed his own.

That night a dream forced him from sleep, the after-images of an old woman holding the knife with the jigged bone handle. He remembered waking up and in a morphine vision seeing the old woman go down on her knees and watching her as she cut the baby from the dying woman to save its life. He remembered the urge to scream or yell or sob, and did so, and afterward Lew asking him if he was okay.

The sheets were sweat through and knotted in his fists and when he woke up the pillow was bloody from his wounded face and he was more tired than before he had slept. He let himself remember the autumn, up through the dusty country where a little girl in a red skirt and white blouse picked a blade of grass and offered it to him.

However much he tried, this night he could not hold back the memories. Sharp and bitter and severe, his dreams were the memories he refused to have. He remembered Tex was in the snow when he found him and he was being knifed to death. He leaped on the man and they rolled in the blood-spattered drift. He fought the man, hand to hand, getting ahold of him and not letting go, but he could not kill him. He bit into the man's face and held him with his teeth and stuffed his .45 in the man's nose and pulled the trigger. The man's blood and bone exploded into his mouth and Henry choked and he tried to swallow and his craw seized and he puked and then he could breathe again, but Tex lay dead in the snow.

On the next hill a marine, called Ski, had his entire abdomen shot away and his spine was revealed and the talons of his ribs, white as dove. And when the overwhelmed enemy tried to surrender, Lew said, we don't take prisoners, and he emptied a clip into them.

He remembered an explosion and then Whitey, a foolish grin on his face, was walking in his direction and waving a hand at him. A claw of flying steel had torn off his other arm.

Slim's legs were pulpified, and before they could get to him he put a pistol to his own head and pulled the trigger. Chief walked off a cliff and another man just up and left.

"Let him go," Henry said when Lew tried to stop him.

"Leave, then," Lew said, and the man set down his weapon and walked away. After that there was just him and Lew and now Lew was dead.

There was light behind the clouds that morning. By the time he made his coffee the sun was out and bright in the sky and the snow was melting away.

He wanted to say something more to Adelita. He wanted to tell her how much he loved her and he would be back. He touched a pencil to his tongue and then to the paper and his hand ran out the words. He left the note on the table where she was most likely to see it when she returned in the evening.

Chapter 38

HE WALKED THAT DAY into night and his mother's letter came back to him again and again. In the streets and doorways in the bad weather there was grace that appeared in the faces of the men and women he saw. The cold air smelled of leaves, opening buds, and soon the heavy smell of the lilacs. Soon the snowball bushes would mass their white blossoms in pink and lavender.

He found the light in the boathouse and could see the city's lights flattening on the water's surface, a path to where thin lines of the water's current pearled and sparkled. He crossed over the beclouded darkness of the river, where all night long were the murmurations of vapors, ghosts, and mists and climbed the bluff and followed down the switchback streets that led in the direction of the boathouse.

He left the streets and waded through drifts of wet rotten leaves as he followed a line perpendicular to the fall of the mountain. Below his traverse was rock faced, slashed up, gullied land with trees draped in kudzu and then the river and beyond the river was the city.

He lost the smell of the river and then he could smell the river below. Under the bluff were the somberest shadows of most neutral twilight. He traversed the steep wooded slope and walked out of the shadow of the trees. A tug was passing by, silently plowing the waters. Smoke from the tug's funnel traveled in the air. The ground was soft with pine needles.

He climbed a railing onto a long staircase and he descended to enter the porch shadows at the back of the boathouse where inside was a light. There were potted begonias and geraniums on the perimeter of the little deck and on the railings were petunias growing in square white boxes.

He waited.

He reflected on the times when things seemed utterly unbearable and now realized that he had been born into them and lived through them. He would live through this also.

He knocked on the door to the boathouse. Someone inside was stirring. He stood at the door and waited and watched east the disappearing view of the river. A light went on.

"Hello?" said a woman's voice. "Who's there?" she said.

Noiselessly, the curtains separated and Mercy appeared at the door, her white shirt blued in the moonlight.

"It's me," he said softly, and stepped back. Mercy stepped outside and into the night with him. Beyond them in the darkness came a whippoorwill's call and then the banging sound of a train taking up slack.

"Where have you been?" she said.

"I have been to Korea."

"What did you go there for?"

"There was a war."

"I know that," she said.

She'd come from sleep and seemed not surprised to see

him. Her face was soft, almost childlike and this night seemed to exist in a trance of delight.

"It's a beautiful night," she said.

"It's as dark as Egypt," he said.

"Do you think there's life out there?" she asked. The moon was filling with light as she spoke of it.

"Sometimes I wonder if there's life right here."

"I am sorry about your mother," Mercy said. "It was a sad thing to've happened."

Seeming to have returned from a distant place, she touched at his face.

"Is it really you," she said.

"Yes," he said.

"No one would tell me where you were," she said, her face blued in the starlight.

At the river's edge a cold vapory mist twined over the tracing water. He closed his eyes to hold back his tears. He imagined his mother in her garden.

"Your poor face," she said. She leaned into him and smiled and when she smiled her wet eyes narrowed.

"I am sorry about your brother," Henry said. "I shouldn't've done that."

"Don't tell me that. I would've wanted you to kill him."

"I only wish I could have met you better in life," he said.

"What's better?" she said.

How could he reply? He lifted his hand and gestured the infinite. She spoke the truth. He clasped his hands behind his back, one hand holding the wrist of the other.

"You're my wandering Ishmael of the Genesis," she said.

Then she said, "There is someone I want you to meet," and she went inside and when she came back out she was carrying a baby wrapped in a blanket. The baby was new and fragile, as if the beginning of knowledge itself. She held the baby out to him, indicating that he should take her in his arms. He unclasped his hands and held the baby in the crook of his arm.

Mercy took his hand in hers and touched his finger to the baby's forehead. He touched the baby's hand and the baby wrapped her small fingers around one of his.

"She's like a little doll," she said. "As soon as you lay her down she falls asleep."

She put her hand up to the back of Henry's neck and held it there as if he was a baby with a baby's weighted skull. She turned his face to look at her.

"She is yours," she said. A star was rising in her eye.

"Mine?"

"Yours and mine," she said. She spoke as if to disclose what was to be kept secret, but no longer.

"Say what you want," she said.

"I can't."

"Whisper it to me," she said, and leaned into him.

"I still love you," he whispered, and he felt the way you feel when you say words you have always wanted to say in your life, to have someone receive them.

"Please stay," she said, and took his hand and led him inside the boathouse, the single room, long and projecting over the river and a staircase to the boat below. It was warm and smelled of wood and the river and the sparrowlike smells that attend a baby in its nursery.

Mercy held on to him by the back of his belt as he let the baby down into her crib. He could feel the heat of her. She put her hand inside his jacket and began to unbutton his shirt.

"I want you to stay with us," she said, and he turned and gathered her in his arms. He then reached down and slipped his arm behind her knees. He lifted her and held her to his chest. Her head fell to his shoulder where she breathed into his open collar. She seemed to grow lighter in his arms, or rather, he became stronger in his carrying of her and she weighed no more than falling rain.

"You can put me down now," she said.

Henry set her on her feet. Mercy took his face in her hands and turned it side to side so she might look at it. Then she drew him to her and kissed him.

"I love you," he said, and she didn't say anything for the longest time.

"I love you too," she finally said. "I love you too," and his heart was as if pierced by a thorn.

"Come into the bed," she said, and the feel of her skin was shocking to him and he could not catch his breath for all of that time.

Her body was soft and pliant and once she had received him with a sigh and a gasp, she surrounded him with her body. He could feel the beating of his heart against hers. There was the faint whisper sound of the water.

"Don't be afraid," she said.

And afterward, when he went to move, she held him, her ankles crossed over his legs. He felt her hand tracing his back and the slide of her foot along his leg. She shifted her hips and held him tight and then he felt her release him and he slipped from inside her.

"I don't sleep good," he said. Then he slept for a while and was not unhappy waking up beside her. She climbed up and lay on his back and he felt the warmth and weight of her body. He felt her fingers on his back, his letheless skin. She traced the cicatrix of the wounds made by the phosphorous and then she touched the compass rose between his shoulder blades and he felt the flat palm of her hand as she rested it there.

Morning was only a few hours away. Beside them the baby girl slept peacefully.

"How did you make it back?"

He told her how he was left behind and so he went back north and was taken in at a logging camp. He told her they used maggots to treat the burns on his back and plaster of Paris. Then they smuggled him to the coast and one night he was taken off in a boat.

"There was some more than just me," he said, and then he said, "Do you think that God being God, that he loves the devil too?"

"It's God's business who he loves and doesn't love."

"Sometimes I think God looked the other way and forgot about us."

"But then he looked again and brought you home."

"It's hard living without the war."

She finger combed his hair. The hair on his right temple had turned white.

"Sometimes you think what you have seen is going to haunt your soul for the rest of your life."

"It must have been so horrible.'

"Don't say that," Henry said.

"Why?"

"Because I was there and I did horrible things too."

"But it wasn't your fault.'

"It doesn't matter," Henry said.

He thought, maybe the telling would break the spell of his long dream. He thought, maybe he was really dead. He said these things to her and watched her face.

"I died every day," he said.

"You have seen too much," Mercy said.

"Yes . . . I have."

"You aren't going to leave me just yet, are you?"

"I will eventually need to go."

"I don't want to hear it."

"I have to go back."

"If I try harder, can I change your mind?"

"No."

When he turned to her again she was smiling, but he knew she was sad. He knew she wanted him to stay. She laced round him with her arms and legs and held him tight and motionless, her face wet with her tears against his shoulder.

"What if I said please?"

The room was warm. He could smell her. He could smell them.

"Take me outside," she said.

Hand in hand they stepped into the last moonlight, their bodies white with glow. The moonlight shined its path on the water and in all of its amplitude was as if the radiance of heaven come to earth.

Down by the river a constant breeze came off the water. Weeping willows lined the banks and shaded the earth and water. He was almost cold. Inside he felt a twist and a tremble and fought back the quaking of his being.

"Do you know what I feel for you?" she said.

"We were young," Henry said, and she looked at him strangely.

"Ours is a love story," she said. "I do not care about anything else."

The stars were fading in the sky. In the east the gray lifting mantle of night and a kindling of pale rose and silver that lengthened and brightened along the horizon. The dark green sluggish flow gave way to darkling pools and placid stretches and the world of living things. The sun was coming up. A sorrowful wind swept in and disappeared.

"I have nothing," Henry said.

"I don't want anything," Mercy said.

"I thought I would never see you again."

"Those were the best days," Mercy said.

"Yes, I think they were."

"I have to go back," he said, and Mercy agreed and said she would wait again forever. He told her she did not know what she was agreeing to.

"I'll miss you when you are gone," she said. "We'll both miss you."

"There'll be more room in the bed when I'm gone."

"I do not know how to let you go," she said. "Not again. When do you leave?"

"Two more days and I have to go."

"Then we will wait here for you."

They went back to the bed and there was still so much to talk about, but a weariness had descended and try as he might, he could not hold off sleep. He slept for a time and when he awoke she was in the rocker beside the bed nursing the baby girl. They were sleeping and yet the rocker still moved ever so quietly. He reached out to rest his hand on her knee where light from the window was draping her left leg. He let his head back on the pillow.

The room was still as glass. When she stood, he slid over and she settled the baby inside his arm and between them. They felt each other in the darkness, their lives come back to them.

She took his hand and held it to her bare skin, moving it from place to place, then kissing each of his fingers, and he felt the rise and seep of her body's sweet waters, the fast blood inside his own body and he began to cry silently. She touched at his scarred cheek. She wiped away his tears. She was saying his name, a messenger calling. The quiet deepened and halfway between sleep and waking he could hear the low, same-changing voice of the water flowing beneath them.